The Desert Store Series

Book Two

The Red Cactus Desert

Geena and the '59 Dodge Lancer

By Patsy Stanley

More books by Patsy Stanley:

Novels:
Addition Jones
An Older Wine
Emerald Hawks Flight
Avalon Blue's Quest

Illustrated books for all age readers:
Christmas Stories From the Crone's Castle
The Dreadful Noises of Landoshar

Native American:
Red Leaf
The Green Mountain Shaman

Metaphysical book Series:
The Mental Body
The Spiritual Nature of Atomic Structure
Sound Energies
Shield Energies
Chakras, Meridians, and the Color Energies
The Elements

The Desert Store Series:
Book One:
Cowboy Johnson's Desert Oasis
Mama and the '57 Mercury

Book Two:
The Red Cactus Desert
Geena and the '59 Dodge Lancer

Book Three:
The Three Cactus Limbo
Bud's Garage and the Quest of the Three Magi

Book Four:
Susan Sugar Diamond
Away in a Desert

"In another time and place, you and I, were."

P.S. Normaine Red Bear, in this book you got your man.

Table of Contents

Chapter One

Hey baby, where da' fancy red dress
I laks' fer' ya' ta' wear?
don't say dat', baby,
Cardinuls' is jist' pretty red birds, baby,
nothin' significant of sin,
I admire yo' long red nails, baby,
'cause the blues ain't the only place we been.

Cowboy Johnson finally told us about the red cactus at the campfire after he and I dealt with the woman in red. I watched him pick up his drawing stick and start drawing cactus shapes in the sand around the fire. I knew he was only sharing his secret with us because of the dangerous woman that stopped at the store for gas. I bet he would have kept the red cactus his personal secret forever if she hadn't stopped; like a whole bunch of other secrets I suspected he kept stashed away.

The woman dressed in red showed up at noon. Everyone was off doing something else, except for Cowboy Johnson and me. She coasted her dusty fire engine red 1953 Austin Healy 100 to a stop in front of the gas pumps and crawled out, clutching a stubby black pistol in her hand. It looked like dull rubber. Not a pistol to admire. Utility. Probably didn't make much of a sound when it was fired. I was standing on the front porch, busy impaling a dead bug with a long pin, readying it for a specimen box. I stopped what I was doing to admire the little red sports car. Then I spotted the ugly gun in her hand.

Puzzled, I looked from the gun to the woman. At first I thought they were tattoos on her face. She wore low slung, tight red, shiny pants with a low-cut red top showing almost all of her breasts and skyscraper red high heels. She was very blond. The kind of color that comes in those bottles in the back of the drugstore.

I watched Cowboy Johnson step out of the garage. He kept wiping his hands on a grease rag as he moseyed toward the gas pumps real slow, taking his time, like he didn't have a care in the world. His steps slowed to a stop about ten feet away from her.

My skeletal joints groaned with tightness and tension as I realized the woman was black and blue, not tattooed. Beat up. Fresh. Eyes full of blood and yellow pain. I wanted to shout her pain because I could feel it. Like Mama, I'm a psychic, too. And yes, for me, pain comes in colors, sometimes too many colors at once, depending on its depth and how quick it comes on. And yellow pain, like hers, is always bad. One of the worst because it is bone deep, attaching itself to the traumas of the persons genetic ancients.

See, everybody around here thinks I'm too immature to understand a damn thing. Their ridiculous point of view wears my patience and my mostly positive attitude pretty thin at times. I guess they expect me to be immature forever, like Mama. Maybe they think Sight is an immature thing to have, but they're wrong. Having the Sight is a troubling gift, a double whammy of a gift. Sometimes it saved, healed, whatever, and you suddenly became a wise woman, a heroine. Most of the time, you ended up looking like an ineffective ass.

I studied the woman's aura. It was full of fire, flaming outward far more than the usual foot it did when people got upset. Her inner child played with matches. A lot. The thickness of her aura told me this woman lived her life stuck mostly in anger mode. It was hard on everybody when someone got stuck using just one emotion to meet all of life's situations when there were dozens more appropriate to choose from, and countless combinations available.

The woman leaned against the hood of her tiny red car and motioned to Cowboy Johnson to fill her gas tank. He circled past her to the gas tank and began to fill it. She watched him, the gun lowered to her side. She stared at him. I could hear her thoughts. He was a man. And a man had inflicted this brutality on her. Her anger rose. The hand with the gun in it rose. She would definitely shoot him if I didn't intervene.

My Sight kicked in. I grew angry. I wanted to run down the steps and do judo on her, kick her ass, though I didn't know how. I wanted to kick the gun out of her hand with a hearty yell. "Ha!"

She looked up at me. I stared into her eyes and visualized her bruised face as having beautiful tattoos on it with landscapes filled with both Dark and Light. I reminded her soul that she had gone through countless rituals in her past lives in which she was gifted with the power those tattoos carried, that to understand this beat up meant that in this lifetime there was no access to the spiritual beautification rituals she needed. Instead, they had gathered force in her unconscious, and given to her in this uninformed, violent way.

Someone named Perry flashed into my mind. He was the only man she loved. Would ever love. Pity flashed through me and was gone instantly. I sent her a telepathic photo of him. He looked like Cowboy Johnson. Perry whoever he was, didn't want the woman to hurt, or for her to hurt anyone else. Especially Cowboy Johnson, for some reason. Puzzled, I backed off and waited tensely while she took in that information. She was having a hard time with it, so I brought the water element in to dim down the fire. It didn't work. It just made her madder. Steamed her up.

I tried to stay focused on her, but something more kept being shown to me. A stand of red cactus nearby. I didn't know anything about a stand of red cactus. What did it mean? My Sight used a lot of symbols, and sometimes it was hard to tell what they meant. There was no time left to find out. I was to direct her to them. They liked and ate anger? Oh well. I caught a sudden glimpse of the red cactus. There were only a few, and they were weird looking. Flat and funny. Something was wrong with them.

"The red cactus desert," I stated loudly into the thick, hot air. Cowboy Johnson gave an imperceptible nod. He didn't realize he'd nodded, but for some reason, unless he agreed, the woman in red couldn't be sent there.

I sent the woman a psychic message to hurry to the red cactus. She didn't have good boundaries or defenses, which is how she got stuck in anger mode in the first place. She eased back into her car and sped off without noticing Cowboy Johnson again. He stood there with her gas cap in his hand. After a long minute, he turned and looked at me, his face pale, eyes silver-green chips of granite.

"Wow!" he breathed, pulling off his cap with the moose logo on it, wiping his face with the back of his hand. He weaved unsteadily toward the porch steps, made it up two of them, and sat down. I wobbled down the steps and thumped down beside of him. He watched the highway. I knew it was in case she came back.

"You saved the day, kiddo. I would have been a goner without you."

I grabbed his arm in a death grip and gasped accusingly.

"The exudations from that damned juniper tree."

I waved my other hand at the lone skinny branch sticking out just past the corner of the store.

"...that thing stinks like a feral varmint in heat on a lonely back road after a deadly forest fire heated it and all its kin into defensive perspiration... just like Mrs. Barry's back unwashed, unleashed, flea bitten dog back home! The damn tree is a pungent, pimply assed, pissy dimorphic juvenile among trees!" My tone was scornful. He didn't ask who Mrs. Barry was.

"That bitch!" I shouted, and promptly threw up. He held me. When I was done, he stood and helped me up the steps, into the store, and into the back room where he planted me on the Hideous Green Sofa. Then he grabbed the rifle he kept propped against his weird looking dresser by the closet door. He hefted it and glanced at me.

"Stay inside."

He meant it.

"Just in case she comes back."

He left, locking the back door behind him. I listened to him lock the front door. Then there was only silence. I sat there, thinking about Cowboy Johnson. I had almost lost him this morning. It happened so fast. We can lose someone we love in an instant. Someone who is our foundation, our bedrock.

I remembered the first time I met him. He was no stranger to me—hadn't been for many lifetimes. I was beyond thrilled to see him again. Maybe now somebody with some common sense would help me out. I circled him and sniffed his Goodness. My new daddy! He didn't know it yet, but I planned to stick to him like glue, forever. Forever Velcro. Mama looked like she'd seen a ghost when she met him. But that was Mama. We both have the Sight. She's the one who started calling him Cowboy Johnson. She seemed to think that was his real name. We started calling him Cowboy Johnson too because he liked it when Mama called him that. Maybe he kept secrets too like the rest of us; maybe he didn't want his real name bandied about in case any robbers of spirits came around.

Maybe he talked about his secrets in that journal he wrote in every night. I often watched him and wondered. When he put on his thick-rimmed black glasses to go over the store's receipts and bills, I knew he would write in the journal when he was done with them. It was the last thing he did every night. I yearned to ask him if there were more journals and could I read them, but I never dared.

Mama was in love with him and he was in love with her. She didn't seem to notice that he loved her back. Mostly she was that way with me, too. When I was little, it used to bother me.

Mama read every book ever written on how to become enlightened, and she studied me speculatively when I was young. I read some of those books of hers to find out what she was up to, and discovered that some of the holy men in those books sit perfectly still in one spot for maybe forty years and subsist on one bowl of rice per day. If a normal mother birthed a kid who chose that spiritual path, she would be devastated, not to mention bored to death by the little brat; but not Mama.

If she'd birthed a son instead of a daughter, he might have been in a predicament. What kind of conversation could a mother have with a kid like that? How was your rice today, son? How about a pot of flowers to liven up the place?

Anyway, that kind of life might be appropriate for many manly spiritual beings that never yearn to have babies or clean a kitchen, but it was not my cup of tea. I wanted to grow up and travel the world and see the pyramids and dance many dances and live near the ocean, which I have never seen. That was it for now. I knew I would change, it was only biological, and I could add more things to my to do list later.

The afternoon crawled by. Cowboy Johnson came and went in the store, carrying his gun, locking the door behind him each time. I was bored out of my terror into sheer boredom by three o'clock in the afternoon and started painting a lizard at my workstation in the store just outside of Cowboy Johnson's living quarters.

Normaine and Mama came home from the ranch with the rest of the misfits at six, hungry for dinner and laughing. Neither of us said anything about the lady in red.

"Come on. Let's go for a short ride," he said to me. I nodded. I knew where we were headed. And it wasn't into Pico Pistachio to get tacos, either. We were headed to Washman's Draw. When we got there, we got out of Elsie, his El Camino, and looked around. There were fresh tire tracks and footprints in the sand. The woman in red came here, then left. Her tire tracks led back out to the highway, curving in the opposite direction from the store. We both gusted out sighs of relief. I started to follow her footprints over the ridge, but Cowboy Johnson called me back.

"Later."

That was all he said. When we got back to the store, I watched him throw away the gas cap she'd left behind. Then he got back in Elsie and took off again. A little while later, he returned with William the Dude following him. They got out and walked off together, talking in low, secretive voices. Then William the Dude left in his gorgeous canary yellow pick up, which I had nicknamed Parry Y. Truck, Parry being short for Parrot, and Y for yellow.

In an hour or so, Cowboy Johnson went out to the campfire grounds behind the store and started the fire. It was too early, but no one seemed to notice. After the fire was going good, I sat down on a log and waited. The rest of the misfits straggled out and joined us. When everybody was accounted for, Cowboy Johnson spoke. He shoved his words out in a reluctant rush.

"There is a hidden place just over the ridge at Washman's Draw. I made it for William so he would have a place close by to drop off the anger and pain from his arthritis. And whatever else. That way, he could unload it and come back into the world quicker."

He shrugged.

"It's the only place I know of where the red cactus grow. There are just a few of them. Their skin is red. They are flat, wide, short and sturdy, with many long red bristles. They have two raised arms with knobby fists at their ends making make them look like they're shaking their fists at something. They are hidden from the highway by the terrain on purpose. They are there to eat people's anger. It is a delicious dessert to them, and a fine fertilizer. Their regular diet is the anger pouring out of the cars and big rigs whizzing by just over the ridge. That is their survival anger. But they like more. They are partial to shouted words and bullets for aeration or eradication purposes. Throwing stuff at them is beneficial too. Today, for the first time, I sent someone there besides William, with Geena's prompting."

He kept drawing cactus shapes in the sand while everyone looked at me curiously. Then he said, "Life hasn't been a picnic for any of us. So next time you get a mad buildup, you might want to go feed it to the red cactus just over the ridge at Washman's Draw."

Everyone looked at each other with puzzled looks on their faces. Then they started laughing.

"You're kidding, right?" they chorused.

Cowboy Johnson didn't crack a hint of a smile. He shook his head no.

"Geena, you go first. You got the right. You earned it today. The rest of you just wait here a few minutes."

It was just a couple miles, but I was a runner, and proud of it. I jumped up and took off running. At last I raced over the ridge. I skidded to a stop and put my hands on my knees and panted while I looked the red cactus over. There were six of them. They stood a few feet apart in a long row, their bottoms buried in sand. They were faded red wood cutouts painted a fresh, fire engine red once upon a time. I started laughing. They looked ridiculous! Each one was stuck in a metal milk can filled with sand and propped upright with two-by-fours. I made out the faded outlines of angry faces painted on them. Their fists were doubled up, punching air. They were riddled with bullet holes. Ridiculous!

Then I stopped laughing. The air here was charged with something. An indestructible, tough smell of robust dill mixed with the sweaty strength of wily road warriors mixed with mummified roadkill and steaming asphalt, rose up around the red cactus in pure, practically holistic, badass vapors. Bad ass courage and kick ass goodness slid through the air and surrounded me. I breathed it in, straightened up and planted my feet wide apart. So, William the Dude comes here to ease his hurt and pain and frustration? Had he shot the bullet holes in the red cactus?

I cocked my head and looked at them, remembering the final road trip Mama and I took to get away from up north. It seemed so long ago. In this place, I knew the memories of the years before the trip were somehow manageable. We'd traveled south down dirt roads that sometimes narrowed down into lanes almost choked to death by weeds in places; places where Mama stopped and backed up and got us out of there. She always said we weren't ready to stop when we just got started. There was no going back. The little, winding road leading to Washman's Draw was kind of like that. You'd never notice it unless you knew it was there. But it was clean and clear and led here.

Maybe I could tell the red cactus desert about the so called "dad" I left back in Ardenville. I just might do that sometime. That way, Mama would never know because I knew she would never come here.

Chapter Two

Ah' runs down 'round da' corner,
my beads clankin' in the night air,
dere's shaderr's sneakin' round, oh yeah,
til' dey' hear the sound of prayer
and my skinny ankles clickin' an' a' movin' on.

Mama told me stories about the Elementals when I was a little girl. One story was about how birds behaved in this world. I never heard that story again. I think she made it up because flight was a large part of her nature. She said that once upon a time, all little girls possessed the souls of birds. The proud girls were like blue jays. They wore showy plumage and gossiped and liked to be mean and didn't like thinkers and took over all the bird feeders.

Then there were girls like robins. They got up early because they were day birds. Early birds. They worked hard during the day and wore red vests to show their industrious nature, stayed sober, didn't understand cleverness or jokes, held solemn gentleness in their souls, sang in church lofts, and wished everyone well.

The little brown sparrows acted and looked like humble little birds when they were alone. But get them together in flocks, and they could tear loose the strongest and biggest of bad, unseen entities that got a hold of people's souls. They could grab and tear away the bad things dwelling in scary places and inside of people and carry them away. The sparrows knew how to use their sharp little beaks and shrieks when the time came right for action. They had the power and sound group Sight carries when it stands together to protect Goodness. They banded together when their own personal world was too small for them to accomplish a necessary powerful act of Sight alone. They acted in community for their spiritual purposes but nested modestly and calmly by themselves otherwise.

Mama said owls were night birds. They were wise with the wisdom the Moon gifted to women. Owls knew how to soar noiselessly in the night, learning things day sounds would have prevented. Owls soared in the night, like eagles soared in the day. Owls and eagles never got personally involved, although they needed each other to open up the days and nights in this world. Owls were the teachers of flying through night skies far up into the heavens where the stars and Moon and planets waited in eternal silence for visitors. They were silent escorts of night flights into dream worlds and the places where unborn hopes lived.

I asked Mama about eagles, but she said she didn't understand them. She told me the traits and powers of many other birds, but I liked the owls best. She said I liked them best because they were old souls and I was one too.

*

I learned to draw snowflakes under the Shadows from Mama. I saw them because I was born with the Sight too. She said we drew snowflakes together under Shadows many times during the darkest nights of our many lifetimes, so we knew the ropes now. We knew the sun would come up for sure, and we could sleep and rest then. But because we carried the Sight, we remembered how the stars, long ago, forged forgotten paths leading to them, and we would forever know those paths and follow the starlight. We could and would solve any problems the Shadows brought us. Others would solve the problems that the light of day brought. Not us. That was not our area of expertise. Mama said we were both Turtle and Owl Clan. Turtle Clan because we lived on Mother Earth and She was the living being providing life for us, and Owl Clan because we were forced to deal with the Shadow this lifetime.

*

"Do lady bugs stay awake at night, Mama?" I asked her.

"No, honey. They sleep in the night, but the black dots on them look like wide open eyes, so the things that would eat them think they are awake and leave them alone."

Mama bought me a book on ladybugs. It didn't take me long to assign attributes to them. She bought me more books and I assigned character attributes and weaknesses to the bugs and birds roaming our little town. I left the dogs and cats out of it. Not interested. In fourth grade, I discovered lizards and science books, added them to the other books, and have been learning about them ever since.

Now that I am a scientist, I now know that the days and nights of my beginning up until I was twelve, were based in Mama's Science School of Survival where Sight reigned, and Sensitives passed through the halls of life like pale shadows. We were both.

*

Mama was naïve, soft and pretty, forever too young to be a mother. She wasn't strict or organized or structured. She never looked ahead to the future and set out rigid plans for it. She just stumbled along. Somehow, she always managed to avoid the inevitable cruelties that harden people's souls, causing them to small down and forget the incredible Bigness they lived in, and why they were here. Mama never collected the meanness causing people to forget about the playing their wise internal child knew how to do; she absolutely trusted it to steer Life away from the waiting Shadow places.

But the Shadow found us, like it did all people, and every now and then, Mama took me and tried to flee from it. My father's Shadow ruled our lives with a steel grip until I was twelve. That I was nearing that transformative age where I could have babies finally woke her up, and we took off in her '57 Mercury for a faraway place—one my father couldn't find.

*

It was a long time since the last time we took off, and I was determinedly settled into the bitterness of thinking I didn't matter to Mama anymore. At least until I searched her face, white with determination to get us away from him, as she set about packing and organizing everything in a way I have never seen her do since. I realized she must have given this escape

21

more thought than ever before. When we ran before, we were forced to come back. Punishment followed.

Mama explained as she packed. "Look. I'm stupid, okay? I always hid too close to here when we left before. That's how he found us and brought us back. This time we're leaving the whole damn state! He is scared to death of leaving this state or going to jail. Those two things give us a chance now that your dumbass mother has finally put it together. It's the last chance we got, kiddo! Get ready! Let's go!" she urged.

I looked at her. There was a finality to her, making hard edges around her usual softness. I knew if we were ever going to escape, it was going to be now. My Sight kicked in.

"The pine trees here stink like old Mrs. Wolley's mean, half dead, mangy, flea bitten, toothless old dog. It likes cloves like HE does, so dump cloves around the outside of both doors so he can't find us. He can smell fear and likes it and can trail it psychically. And old Mrs. Wolley's reeking, mangy, old fuzzy dog stinks like a skunk in heat on a hot Saturday afternoon in late August, like the pines do in protest of its dog house being under them, like his is here, so pour some of that pine stuff stored under the kitchen sink around the bed he sleeps on. Don't dilute it. I guess the dog and He can't help themselves, but I don't want anything more to do with them."

Mama nodded; her face bent to her task. I grabbed my things and threw them into cardboard boxes and paper grocery sacks. My father burned our suitcases and dared us to get any more. We pulled together and filled the Merc' as fast as we could. Everything was in place. We'd done this before. When we were finished, we removed all traces leaving clues for him to find. We didn't know where we were going. Away from him was good enough. She spread the cloves, poured the pine oil, and we were off. Headed out of Ardenville. On the lam again.

I stared out the back window as the clock that towered over the town disappeared. Good riddance. It was part of the brick factory where most of the people in Ardenville worked. Mama started working in the factory beneath it shortly after I was born.

By the time I was twelve, I was raising Mama. There was too much I couldn't do as a kid. My childhood ended when I was about four out of necessity, so Mama became the adult who did things for the kid who was raising Mama.

When I wasn't raising Mama, I was out looking at bugs. But I didn't collect them because my Sight informed me to beware! They would pull my father down into an even lower life form than the scummy, sneaky, hairball he already was. Besides, Mama was terrified of him and them.

When I turned twelve, Mama and I put an inside lock on my bedroom door for a birthday present while my father was gone somewhere. I achieved this wondrous happening by searching out books on the needs for adolescent privacy at the library, then bringing a huge stack of books home and leaving them laying around the house. I knew Mama would read them because she read everything from soup labels to fortune cookies. I knew my semi-illiterate father would pass them by without a glance. The stage was set. Mama was my only chance.

Mama read the books with my father breathing heavily over her shoulder, looking avidly at the pictures, trying to distract her. But nothing on God's green earth ever deterred Mama from her books; not even him. And he knew it. She read them all and agreed that I needed my privacy because I was "growing up."

Next, following my plan, I sweetly and timidly asked her for a bedroom door lock in front of my father, who couldn't tell her the real reason he didn't want me to have one. He went somewhere, we went to the store, got the lock, brought it back, put it on. It worked. Window locks and door locks and ignoring the muted tapping on the door and the whispered threats. I was safe until he figured out his next move. I knew beyond a doubt he'd find a way. I planned to run away on my own before that event occurred. But I didn't have to, because here we were again, on the lam.

I felt like crying and sniffled. Mama heard me.

"What are you crying about?" she asked in a huffy voice. "I thought you'd be happy to leave..." she said without finishing her sentence.

We both knew what she left unsaid.

"No. It's grandma. I'm gonna' miss her."

"Oh."

"Well, me too," she said after a minute.

Grandma was the only person I ever trotted out my leftover childhood self in front of. She's the reason I still have one.

I smoothed the leather of the back seat with my hands. Everyone said my hands were like grandma's. I was leaving again without learning more from her. Mama said grandmas Sight sprang from Fortitude. I watched the way my grandfather and uncles made fun of her. But their uppity attitude gave her the freedom to go her own way as long as she did it in a court jester sort of way.

She told me so when I tried to join in with them and belittle her for her "silly" ways. I scoffed and she said, pulling her hair back and smoothing it into a ponytail with lines of silver running heavily through it, "Sometimes you can do more with honey than with vinegar, though they are both advisable to use in different situations."

I cocked my head up at her, admiring the silver wings at her temples for a minute. She stood still and let me admire her. Then she grinned and grabbed my arm. "You stick with me today." It was an order—a command. There were other plans percolating in my mind, one of them being the advancement of my psychic abilities through learning the art of levitation. Anything for freedom.

My plans were forgotten while I watched her skip nimbly in and out her effective, familiar roles. The Mother, nodding and smiling, the Wife, nodding and smiling, the Cook, nodding and smiling, the solemn Wise Woman practicing the art of Awe while we hid in the garden, the Deflector waving a dishcloth as a shield, the Court Jester steeped in pretended grand confusion and helpless anger to satisfy the King and his inhabitants. She didn't need to be any smarter, any wiser, and as I learned that day, she cleverly avoided ever being consigned to the role of being a Great Lady to the King. She simply was who she was and enjoyed the flexibility it gave her.

"How do you do it?" I asked in wonder.

"I keep my pride bendable and my need to feel offended tamed."

While acting naïve, she wisely and subtly managed to raise a large family without too many mishaps and no real tragedies, skillfully using her many arts of role playing giving others the credit willingly. That part didn't bother her like it bothered me.

Her house was clean and bright with sunlight and white crocheted doilies standing proudly on the backs of the couches and chairs. She stiffened their flounces in sugar water. She showed me how to do it. I still have a doily of hers. I stole it when I was eight. She knew it and didn't say anything.

Whenever I spent the night with her, she fixed me three fried eggs and a pan of biscuits and a pound of bacon the next morning; so much food it took a platter to hold it. She set with me like a girlfriend, of which I had none, and smiled at me while I ate and talked as much as I could.

My Sight informed me long ago that she wanted to do for me what she couldn't do for Mama. She would unlock the doors to her own kind of Sight and let me see it and tell me how it worked if I could stick around long enough. That way, I could learn how to handle my worrisome, stiff pride. Many times, she circled me, inspecting me. One time she said with a frown, "That silly pride of yours has got lumbago again!"

I sucked in my breath.

"What's that?"

"Somethin' like arthritis," she finally said, and walked away. I raced after her. She walked faster and faster. We both ran out the back door. It slammed shut behind us. She ran down the three short steps to the grass and stopped and looked at me inquiringly.

"How's that lumbago? Gone yet?"

I shook my head stubbornly.

"Nope. I'm still mad at Mama."

"Is that a right or a privilege?" she questioned to herself and turned away.

I sighed and gave in.

"How do I fix it?"

"Your lumbago?"

I nodded, though we both knew what she really meant.

"Yes," I answered. I knew better than to just nod. I bent over like a ballerina on one leg. I reached for the sky while I hopped, skipped, and jumped, snorted, whinnied, and clucked, arms flapping. I walked forward, sideways, and backward while snapping my fingers.

We heard voices. Hastily she said, "Okay. That's good enough."

I examined where I was with my lumbago and nodded. It was time to go make up with Mama. I wanted grandma to teach me much, much more, but every time we got started, we were interrupted. Sooner or later, sure as lightning, rain or thunder, grandpa or one of the uncles would come in and order her around. Bark at her. And immediately, her emotional temperature would rise, she'd become flustered and slam the psychic doors shut that were gently opening between us. They laughed at us, as if they knew what we were up to.

I searched in me for how I felt about leaving her. I tried to drum up some sadness, but it wasn't there. I'd known for a long time that her kind of knowing wasn't the same as mine. I sucked in my breath. Two weeks ago, in my dreams, she gave me a small, faded suitcase, tan with yellowed stickers on it. The stickers were from places all over the world. Paris, France. London, England. India. Peru. I guess she hoped I would become a world traveler someday. She laughed and recited a little school poem to me before she left my dream, citing my worst enemy in school in it.

"I see London,

I see France,

I see Kris Maine's underpants!"

Sometimes she winked at me behind everybody's back. She was winking at me now.

Sometimes I wondered what the rest of the ancestral women we came from were like. They managed to put up with men and raise babies to have more babies. I wondered how many of our female lineage became clowns and court jesters and role players, diverters of countless different kinds, jeered at by men, safely playing second best out of a need to insure survival for themselves, their children, and their future generations?

I would never know.

There were only flowers and fences in Ardenville to explain life to me. Very front porch people lived there, one might say. It was a small town where petunias and gladiolas and zinnias blossomed in the sunshine, admired by people passing by, while the Shadows of some of the planters of those flowers hid behind smiles in the houses and waited for darkness. Others knew all about them and looked the other way.

*

So it was that I learned about some of the unseen parts of life long before I became a scientist, before my husband cheated on me and broke my heart, pushing me into learning the smells of different kinds of sages and those of other lands, so I might begin a grounding in how to love in new ways. I needed to learn, you see, because love is an activity, and because every day, I chose to keep him. And though I will always appreciate science, my unseen teachers and my Sight have always stood strong and stalwart within me. When my Sight beckons to me, I answer the call. It is a friend to me and I shall not abandon it, ever. I couldn't if I wanted to.

Çhapter Three

Tell dem' dam' church bells ta' quiet derselves' down!
I still ain't gonna' stay' here!
I gots' my own 'lationship with God ta' tend to.
tain't nobody's dam' bid'ness but ours
and jis't in case you feel like askin'
I got it cause' I roamed around til' I found it...ha ha!

I smoothed my hands over the Merc's back seat. I could count on it to feel cool and large. It was the color of happy, tropical water. The back windows were clean and large, framed with white and chrome and more leather. Mama took excellent care of the Merc'.

Organizing the chaos that living out of a suitcase entails is an acquired skill involving both losses and costs, but it is a skill that forever remains a friend if needed again. I learned this philosophy early on. Mama always bought land yachts. They were her real home. She kept two cans of Campbell's Chicken Noodle soup, a can opener and two spoons under the driver's seat. She stored books, umbrellas, extra coats for us, and a kite for flying in them. She would have stored more, but my father kept an eye on what she put in each car and took out what he didn't want her to have, because he was afraid she would run away again.

At times while I was growing up, he tried to convince me to do away with her. He whispered that she was a nut job and needed locking up or killing. I ignored him. He was the Shadow, and my soul recognized that fact from the start. My angels or god knows who- somebody-protected me from too much emotional bonding with him by giving me probable theories about how this ugly situation came about.

Whoever it was said it was because our past lives were intertwined many times before. This time, my father wanted the power that negative emotional control over me-and others- would give him. Mother's usually bond with their children, but Mama was weak before him because of her fear of his Shadow.

She worked and did all she could, but her spirit couldn't go near him and deal him the blows he needed to be put back on the path of Goodness or destroy him. I could of, and should have hated her, but I didn't. Someone needed to stand against him. Guess who. I was the warrior soul forced into a corner this lifetime with him, because there would come a time when I could kick his ass. And would. I owned the grit, the Sight. It was a David and Goliath situation. No matter what he did to me, against all odds, my soul was intact. Mama kept trying to help me, and that's why I could still love her.

Mama told me many stories about Goodness. My soul did too. It said Mama misread the label I came with. I scoffed when it said all souls came with a description—it ignored my disbelief that she named me wrong. I was supposed to be named Athena after one of the old warrior goddesses, but she got the tag on my halo wrong, and named me Geena instead. But that was all right. Nothing is an accident. I needed a disguise. Just not from myself. I scoffed again. No, my soul insisted. "Every newborn anything has a halo. Some keep them, some don't stay attached to the bigger picture, which is what's required to keep your halo. The outer chakras, you know? Yours is still real strong."

My soul also coolly informed me not to get too shook up; I was not alone in my suffering. It said my mental body needed teaching. It sent me to the library to read about other countries and culture's treatment of females. Many cultures normal lifestyles included female bondage. Some women were for this, most weren't. I was appalled. I wasn't alone. I read about incest and many other forms of power grabbing of innocence by men, relatives, and otherwise of women. I wised up and became smarter about handling my father. I was a pretty damn tough twelve-year-old, thoroughly wounded—and weary—by the time Mama and I ran away from him for the last time.

Mama said she kept things in her cars because she grew up in deep poverty. Her father dragged his wife and children to migrant worker camps where they topped onions, lived in abandoned, falling down houses weathered into silver silence from age and hopelessness, and mostly out of his old cars. They bunched clothes into corners in shacks and slept on them. Mama was nine when they finally moved into the house in Ardenville and put down roots.

Someone gave grandma a rusty, double bed frame and a lumpy mattress when Mama was ten, so Mama and her sisters finally got a bed to sleep on. She didn't like the bed. She said it was rusty with busted springs poking through the lumpy mattress. She slept on the edge of it once in a while, but mostly on the floor. I guess she was used to moving on by then. Maybe she learned to like moving on, maybe that's why she drove cars as big as small motel rooms and talked about traveling.

The life Force. It comes along and pushes you into the next place you need to be, whether you like it or not. My soul said each person has an agenda to be met when they come here. Whether you go easy or fight it, the Force doesn't care. It doesn't care if you have a bed or not. Or a suitcase. It's going to make you move on to the next place anyway. Our little feelings don't matter. Mama calls it Karma.

Every summer Mama and I walked to the annual car show in Ardenville to look the land yachts over. Mama leaned down and whispered, "There are other people like us out there, you see? These are their cars. Aren't they beautiful?"

She meant the people more than the cars. We ate popcorn and stared hungrily at the strangers. "Someday..." Mama always murmured during the three days the car show lasted. But three days was never long enough.

Other people sensed that Mama was unable to connect to them in a way they understood, so they instinctively kept her on the edge of their decisions and situations and not in the mainstream. It hurt her feelings and she stayed puzzled by it. But Mama understood things no one else did. She understood how Nature uses blankets to help the force of Good stay strong. She explained it to me.

"Whatever covers something is acting as a blanket. It is in the Nature of all things to rest at times. Nature uses snow or sand or rain or other things as blankets to change the architecture, to hide and protect the Good when it has to lay down and rest for. That's what we're waiting on."

I frowned at her, puzzled.

"We're waiting on Good to get up from sleeping," she answered in response to my unasked question, as though that explained everything.

That was Mama. She understood things I never thought about. During my troubled childhood, I slowly came to realize that although no one can explain Algebra to an Angel, Mama could be counted on to draw perfectly structured snowflakes under the Shadow just at the right time—every time. In that way, she was absolutely reliable.

Mama's soul lived in God's hands, while I held my soul in my own hands. God could go to Hell for all I cared. He, She, It, or Them were always off somewhere else, maybe playing golf like that one kid in school said. And there was the story that when it thundered, it was God-He-She–It-Them-throwing a bowling ball. If the thunder was particularly loud or long, then God made a strike or spare in that Great Bowling Alley in the Sky. Bull crap. God had all kinds of excuses for not helping us humans. I never shared my beliefs about God with Mama. She would have been horrified.

*

When Mama turned the Merc' onto the first unknown highway far enough away from Ardenville for me to relax, I fingered the secret roll of money in my pocket and allowed myself to hope we might not have to go back for as long as whoever or whatever God was, lived.

How did Bud Spinner know we were leaving? Did Mama tell him? I couldn't ask because of the money in my pocket. Bud Spinner was Good. He was short and stocky with straight brown hair cut into a butch. His eyes changed from sort of brown to green when he looked at Mama. Though they didn't look alike, I could tell they were kin on the soul planes.

Last week when we stopped at Bud's Gas Station for our weekly fill up of gas, Mama got out of the Merc' and went inside, as usual. I knew she was studying the big map pinned up on his office wall. I watched Bud fill the gas tank, then he shoved a wad of money into her purse through the open front passenger window. He did it quick, like the money was on fire. Her latest huge purse squatted on the front passenger seat, brown like a huge, ugly, week old dead troll holding a dead bouquet of flowers. I reached up and grabbed the roll of money out of the ugly thing and shoved it deep into my jeans pocket. Bud watched me with approval. Yeah. We both understood Mama when it came to money.

I wrinkled my nose, sniffed the air and said to him, "There's a rusty orange generator, might burn up soon, over at old man Sedgewick's place. Might happen while he's gone visitin' his brother next week. The curtains on the windows might catch on fire and burn up. Won't kill nobody. But there might not be anything left to cover up the bad stuff he's got hid up at his place anymore."

He studied me a few seconds and nodded.

I nodded back.

"Yeah. Let it happen. You could stop it, but don't."

I said this because maybe Bud was a volunteer firefighter. I didn't know for sure. Best to cover all the bases. Bud went in the gas station and soon Mama came out with a thick, folded paper in her hands. She opened the trunk and put the paper in it. Later I found out it was a map of the United States. I stared out the back window at Bud as we left. He was outside standing by a gas pump, watching us. I didn't wave goodbye because I liked him.

I planned to mix Bud's roll of cash in a little bit at a time with the skimpy bit of money Mama got out of the tin can buried in the back yard. I checked and there wasn't near enough money. That's the way Mama was. That's why my father always found us.

My personal hope and the cash she didn't know about, which had to do with me and Bud Spinner, not God, caused me to make the backseat of the Merc' into a home for myself. A hopeful hotel on wheels. I spread out a blanket, fluffed a couple throw pillows, strategically placed stuffed animals and chips within reach, and made myself comfortable.

I sat back to watch mountains, fields and farms, days and nights, sunrises and sunsets and other parts of life pass by through the windows of Mama's '57 Mercury. Watching the world outside Ardenville during that road trip instilled an awe for life in me I still carry today. It was a gift to an errant, psychic girl on a runaway road trip because she was willing to try moving on one more time.

*

It was a couple of days after we visited California that we stopped at Cowboy Johnson's store out in the middle of Nowhere, in the New Mexico desert. We planned to gas up and grab a couple of cold sodas. We got out and stretched. Mama started toward the store to get sodas and pay for the gas. That's when I saw Normaine Red Deer sitting in Esmerelda. She was crying, and I knew instantly Mama was supposed to help her. Then Cowboy Johnson strolled out of the store to gas up the Merc', and the cooing of doves circled my head—he wore a halo too! I knew I was home now.

Cowboy Johnson reminded me of Bud Spinner. He was short and stocky with straight brown hair. I fclt the Goodness radiating from him like it did from Bud. I looked around. The store and gas station used to be a little white church. There was a mechanic's bay to the right of the store. They both owned garages. Another way they were alike. And that's how I got to meet two more misfit angels out in the middle of a desert in Nowhere, New Mexico—Normaine Red Deer and Cowboy Johnson.

We stayed at the store a couple of days, helping Normaine re-kill her dead husband in a new and everlasting way. His death stuck that time, so we decided to go north with her to Wyoming so she could marry Eddy. It was after Mama and I went north and Mama helped Normaine jilt Eddy that we returned to Cowboy Johnson's store for the second time.

The original plan was to leave Normaine in Wyoming and head back south after her wedding to Eddy. But Mama and Normaine got cold feet and

Mama helped her jilt Eddy before he could get home for their wedding. Eddy was a semi truck driver, and he was on the road most of the time.

When those two started wailing about all the bad men and their suffering, and how they could never love a man or marry again, I took off.. They were busy stabbing the chairs and couch with butcher knives when I grabbed Mama's purse and the Merc's keys. I drove the Merc' into town, booked a room at the hotel, shopped, ate pizza, and took a long bubble bath before they arrived, all dirty and happy.

By the time they got to the hotel, Normaine decided she wasn't going to marry Eddy. Whatever. I helped them replace Normaine's ex-betrothed's furniture and other wares they destroyed in his trailer before we headed back south.

Mama and Normaine started falling apart on the road trip back to the store, so I drove much of the way. At night, we slept in roadside parks full of dangerous vagrants. The two of them wouldn't bathe or comb their hair, and they stunk and ignored anything I said and ate giant bags of potato chips and chocolate.

I drove us into the parking lot at the store, at which point I jumped out of the Merc' and threw myself into Cowboy Johnson's arms. After all, I was only twelve, though my soul protested otherwise. Cowboy Johnson dressed them down, then took care of me while Mama and Normaine retreated into psychic comas. I guess the miles of junk food they ate wasn't enough to keep them from going into stupors.

Cowboy Johnson pumped up an air mattress in his living quarters next to his Hideous Green Sofa and the two of them fell on it like sacks of potatoes and slept forever. When they weren't sleeping, they moved like turtles in slow motion to the front or back porch where they sat speechless, like lumps of clay in rockers.

Cowboy Johnson slept on his cot in the corner while I slept on the Hideous Green Sofa beside the Snoring Ladies. Their level of snoring was that of Chuck Yeager flying the first jet that broke the sound barrier in 1947. Maybe they could become famous too. In self-defense, I dreamed of trussing them to rolling beds of some kind, then shipping them off air mail to a traveling circus charging fees for looking at their comatose, snoring forms blasting and roaring sounds into the night air. No doubt we could afford a mansion in a matter of a few Big Top nights. Cowboy Johnson and I used ear plugs to deafen the sound.

Cowboy Johnson made campfires out back. He played his guitar and toasted marshmallows and fried bologna on sticks for me. And that is how I came to live at Cowboy Johnson's Desert Oasis with my Good father, and later, how I learned about the red cactus desert.

Until we found Cowboy Johnson, Mama and I didn't have a chance of a snowball in hell of ever becoming who we could be, even though we owned the equipment for it. We were just angry, scared, psychic roadies, running away from small town predator Hell.

Chapter Four

Yeah, I got me a big thaing' for dem' designer glasses,
fo' fancy smancy plates, and thin, bony ankles
yeah, yeah, I shure' does
but mostly, it's the color of thaings'
that gives my soul it's flighty, dancy ways!

My Good, real father. For some reason only God and Mama knew about, Mama called him "Cowboy Johnson" right from the start. Her nickname for him caught on with the rest of us and stuck. He seemed fine with it, just a little bit relieved, so we left it alone.

His real name is Avery Mott Judson. It took me years and a lot of pilfering to find out his family was wealthy as old sin, and just about as busy. How he stayed hidden from them was a mystery to me, until I put two and two together, and came up with William the Dude Makepeace. Later, I learned that William the Dude, Cowboy Johnson, Emma, and some of the other store misfits used aliases, all for different reasons.

William the Dude and I met shortly after we moved into Cowboy Johnson's store. William the Dude was slim. He wore wrinkled jeans, run down cowboy boots, and fitted, snap down, faded, blue denim shirts. His lined face was deeply tanned and wrinkled in all the right places. His white hair waved down onto his shoulders, his eyebrows bushy and white above sky blue eyes. His nose was long like a ski slope above a thin, twitchy mouth.

He ambled into Cowboy Johnson's store one morning, and I liked him as soon as he set his light blue eyes, the color of China Sea paint on sale from the Hardware Depot, on me and grinned. I looked him over. He looked like a dusty, ancient prospector who'd given up on finding his pot of gold out there somewhere in the New Mexico desert. I figured him for a prospector who kept going through the motions because he didn't know what else to do. That's what I figured, but I was dead wrong.

"Hello," he greeted me with a grin.

"Hi."

I shortened my greeting to fool him into thinking I was just a kid. I grinned back at him and bowed low, letting my hair fall forward to sweep the sandy floor. My hair was down to my knees, thick and straight. It made a great hiding place. I used my hand to sweep the sand around a little bit with my hair before I remembered that someone existed outside my curtain of hair.

I raised my head and he was still there, head bowed low to me as though he hadn't seen me wandering through my hair. His ice blue eyes twinkled as he straightened up and waited. It was my move. The old dude was giving the kid the first move? That was news, coming from an adult.

In gratitude, I went over to the freezer and took out a purple Popsicle and carried it to him. Grape.

"What's your name?"

"William. What's yours?"

"Geena."

I studied him as words of wisdom came to me.

"Old people should always eat purple."

He nodded and peeled back the paper wrapper.

"No quarrel there. Is that your mom out there on the porch?"

I took an orange Popsicle out of the freezer and peeled the wrapper back for myself, taking my time.

"Why? Do you think we look alike?"

"Well, maybe just a tad."

I cocked my head to the side.

"What's a tad? You mean tadpole?"

He turned with me in my new direction and nodded.

"Tadpoles turn into frogs."

He nodded again.

"Like their parents."

"Which of the two on the porch do you think is my parent?"

"Well, it sure ain't Normaine."

"You know Normaine?"

He nodded.

"Since she was knee high to a gnat."

I snorted.

"Nobody's ever that little!"

"Maybe, maybe not."

Then he asked the big question, the one everybody else always avoided. Only he asked it in way that told me he understood.

"Froze up, are they?"

I stood there blinking at him while he waited for the answer like he had all the time in the world. I liked that he thought I would know what "froze up" meant. And I did. His question described them exactly. I sighed and looked down at the solid plank floor. I tested it with a couple of short jumps. Was it rickety any place? No.

How to explain that Mama and her new sidekick had joined forces and gone off the rails over men problems and were now renegotiating with their innards about them? That they were meditating upon it for what might end up being years to come, maybe the rest of my life, and while it was going on, no one else in the world existed for them? Including me? And that all they needed from me was more junk food while they were stuck in their stupors?

"Been going it alone for a long time, huh?"

His soothing, sort of high voice interrupted my thoughts.

"Since I was born."

The words quavered their way out of me, and I burst out crying. I was immediately horrified at myself. I took care of Mama through thick and thin and never shed a tear. But let the lovely grandfather guy with the gentle voice lovely, fairy tale voice show up, and I turned into a wailing wall.

He put his arm around my shoulder, and I laid my head on him. Anywhere it landed. He stood there, awkward and kind, patting my back and smoothing my hair. A short little cry, and I was through. I moved away, dried my eyes, blew my nose, and peered up at him. He saw the question in my eyes.

"Yep. They'll get over it."

I wanted to ask him to be my grandpa forever, but I was afraid to. He must have heard what I was thinking.

"I'll be around. I bet my ride is ready by now. Want to see it?"

He grinned and motioned to me. I pictured a dusty donkey braying or a ratty old truck on bald tires, but politely kept my mouth shut. We walked the long length of the store together. He opened the screen door and bowed me out.

"After you!"

We minced across the porch, ignoring Normaine and Mama, then pranced daintily down the steps as though we were entering a ballroom to dance. The hood was up on a fabulous canary yellow truck that said GMC on the side of it in a funny silver script. Cowboy Johnson was working under it. I looked around for the no doubt dusty—we were in a desert, right?—old pickup or car he drove. Or even a mule or a donkey. Cowboy Johnson shut the hood on the beautiful truck and turned to William, wiping his hands on a rag.

"Carburetor looks fine. She's all set."

I stared at them, open mouthed.

They laughed.

William said proudly, "She's a customized 1946 GMC half ton EC101 pickup."

I stared yearningly at the gorgeous canary yellow truck. I wanted to take a long, maybe forever ride in it. I wanted to clean its carburetor. I wanted to braid my hair in front of it. Wipe the engine down and frame the oily rag I used. Drive it across desert sands to faraway places with exotic names. I wanted to park it outside of forbidden dance halls and inside of drive-in theaters with buttered, salted popcorn and a tall boy close by my side. I wanted it more than I wanted sparkly red shoes I could click together to make wishes come true.

"I'll see you later."

William opened the truck door and swung up into the cab.

"See you later, William," Cowboy Johnson answered.

I stepped back, then raced up the steps and into the store. His name was William. Now I knew. There was plenty for me to think about. For the first time, somebody else recognized that I was raising Mama and I was too young to do it and knew it, and it scared the living hell out of me. A stranger named William recognized my predicament, didn't judge her or me, and accepted it without giving me the third degree. Now there was Cowboy Johnson, and a new good grandpa to help! More Angels! Hallelujah!

I heard Cowboy Johnson come in. I ran through the store and out the back door. I raced to the campfire and ran in circles around the ashes until I was sweating and panting hard. I bent over and grabbed my knees, getting my breath back. Laughter, gut-rolling, side-splitting laughter, erupted from me. I yelped and howled with exultation. I staggered around, kicking up sand and finally fell to my knees and gave thanks to whoever or whatever it was running my show. They'd finally decided to have a little mercy on me. By the time I got all of my laughing out at this crazy mixed up world, Normaine and Mama were meandering around the house towards me. Cowboy Johnson was standing on the back porch, watching me, holding something in his hands.

I doubled into fresh peals of laughter watching them struggle across the sand towards me at a turtle's pace listing sideways like two lost ships. The second coming of Christ would surely happen before they made it to me! I would be old and have died of natural causes and turned into a mummified skeleton long before they got here! I rushed them and almost bowled them over.

"Argghhh?" they asked in a questioning tone.

"I just met another Angel!" I shouted.

They smiled vacantly at me. I hugged them and petted them and turned them around so they could head back to their seats on whichever of the store porches. Then I ran towards Cowboy Johnson. What was it he was holding? I ran up the steps.

"What is it?"

I skidded to a stop in front of him. He held a large red block in his hands.

"It's clay. Here."

He dumped the dark red blob in my hands. My knees almost buckled from the weight of it. I complained.

"It's a lot heavier than it looks!"

"Don't complain, kiddo! Carry it to the table I've set up for you in the left corner in the back of the store and make something out of it. I put a couple of tools out for you to use. Oh…and read the brochure that came with it first."

He turned and went back inside. I stood there a minute before I followed him. That was my introduction to clay. I cautiously set to work making a little lizard, but it ended up looking more like a pencil with a large eraser for a tail than anything else. Also, it was all red. Where were the colors?

Cowboy Johnson drove me to the library in Pistachio Pico and we checked out lizard books with lots of large, colorful pictures. Soon I was making fairly accurate clay depictions of lizards, birds, little people, and bowls. But how to paint them?

A few days later, I was sitting at my work table in the back of the store, hands under my chin, studying the clay lizard I just finished. The screen door opened. In came the old prospector, William Makepeace, followed by a tall, dark haired, bronzed boy a little older than me. I watched the boy swagger easily across the space between us, his handsome face filled with the assurance of his acceptance anywhere.

"Miss Geena, this is my grandson, Ray Makepeace," the old geezer said.

"Nice to meet ya."

We both said it at the same time. Then we laughed.

"Miss Geena, Ray's mother is my daughter. She is an artist. I told her you wanted to expand your artistic abilities, so she wants to meet you. Would you be willing to go for a ride out to my place with me and Cowboy Johnson? Ray here can stay and mind the store. He's done it before."

"Yes!"

I shouted and jumped up and went into my boogie dance before I could stop myself. Then I screeched to a stop and blushed. What was the matter with me? Rays teeth were lovely, even and white teeth when he smiled. I could smell him from here. A lovely combination of mint and young man sweat. He leaned over and whispered to me.

"Just call him William the Dude like I do."

William the Dude interrupted my thoughts about the loveliness of the flecks of gold in Ray's dark eyes.

"Best collect some of your art into a basket or something, so Emma will know what you might need."

I hastily grabbed the clay lizard I was working on and looked around for a basket.

We reached William the Dude's ranch house after a long ride down a dusty single lane road on a highway turnoff not far from the store. The ranch house looked like a compound. My impressions were of rock and wood and sandstone exteriors. There were nooks, crannies, cactus gardens, wandering paths, and vines clinging to the walls. There were porches and canvas shaded vegetable gardens and walkways muted in earthy colors, shaded, always shaded with ledges, rocks, or canvas.

I followed them through a set of open double doors. They stopped and watched me. I wondered why until I noticed the gorgeous, living color surrounding me, then I forgot all about them. I let out a long, low whistle and turned in slow circles. Gorgeous, deep color everywhere. Lines and squares and shapes of pure color. It was a feast of symmetry and totally kinetic Sight following its own true path of knowledge to amazing endings and beginnings. No middle ground here. No ho hum. Brilliant color everywhere.

Finally the sound of water in a fountain trickling down watery pathways entered my consciousness. I looked around. There was a fountain carved into a far corner of the huge, lofty room. Water trickled over a stack of cleverly placed rocks. Two stories above the waterfall was a smooth, stark white ceiling. I turned in a circle again.

The most amazing color was contained in huge canvases covering all four walls. No landscapes or portraits. Just intense sheets and folds and curves and splashes covering every inch of each canvas, making each one look like it was going to burst its seams with color any second. A flood of color longing to escape into the desert where the empty, living space it deserved anxiously and impatiently waited to suck it in.

Emma Makepeace strolled into the room, small, dark haired and willowy in elegant gray trousers and a white blouse. She emanated a serene radiance. I knew instantly she was soft and given to flying away, like Mama. Another one with Sight, one more interested in the integrity of character and the potential it carried than anything else.

Ray's black eyes, olive skin, and beautiful facial structure were like hers. Miss Emma held out her hand to me and smiled.

"Hildy, please have Betty bring the gentlemen something to drink while Geena and I visit," she said to the lady hovering behind her. She drew me close as we walked out of the room. She said to me in a low conversational tone, "Somehow I don't think the men are interested in the same things we artists are. They like trucks better."

We laughed.

"You may call me Miss Emma," she said.

I left carrying a box of paints, brushes, scrapers, a palette, cleaners, and jars along with instructions from Miss Emma.

"Be here at seven Saturday morning. Bring something to paint and I will teach you more."

"Oh yes! I will! Thank you!"

Back at the store, I set everything out on my work table and began painting lizards, bowls, little people, birds, and other clay things.

I spent Saturday mornings on walking trips through the desert with Miss Emma. She opened my eyes to Nature's grand colors and shadings. Afterwards, we painted in her light filled studio, ate something, then Ray picked me up and drove me back to the store.

After many repaints, I put the lizards and other clay pieces out for sale. I needed to buy more paints and other stuff, and I didn't want to ask Miss Emma for anything more. I was lucky, for everything I made sold out as fast as I could make them. I bought paints and clay with the money and saved some. "You're an entrepreneur now. Save your money for supplies and college, and you will do well," Cowboy Johnson said as he handed me three slim books. I hoped they were some of the journals he wrote in, but they weren't.

"Here are your new account books. I will show you how to use them."

I felt like I was graduating from something. I jumped up from my work table and hugged him. Thank God somebody helped me plan for my future, for there were times when I wondered if Mama would ever come out of her internal obligation research endeavors. And that's how I became an entrepreneur.

*

Normaine got better first and started making rag rugs. She nicknamed herself "Normaine the Ripper," and said she liked to rip the materials apart so their edges were frayed, like hers. She said ripping exorcised the angry part of her. So much for developing a new philosophy while immersed in a coma.

Then Mama started getting better. One day she wasn't on the porch, front or back. She was making her own cheese sandwiches lately too. I found her sitting on the Hideous Green Sofa in cowboy Johnson's living quarters, staring down at her hands.

"Waiting for something to do?"

She peered up at me.

"Aarrgghh?"

That's all she said. *Was she ever going to get better?* I heaved a sigh, turned away and glumly stalked back to my work table. Cowboy Johnson and William the Dude were sitting at the counter, chatting about the weather and other things, drinking root beer. Three large cardboard boxes were sitting at their feet.

"I guess we could give this stuff to the mission people in town."

"I guess so. I'll take them over there."

William the Dude stood up and sighed. I was listening.

"What's in the boxes?" I asked.

"I don't know exactly. Just some stuff old lady Jenson wanted to get rid of," William the Dude answered.

"Humph! There could be a veritable treasure hidden in those simple cardboard boxes!"

I advanced on the boxes with the intent and purpose of searching out hidden treasure.

"Go ahead."

William the Dude and Cowboy Johnson moved quickly out of the way. "Let us know when you're done," they chorused back over their shoulders and left.

The first two boxes held old clothes smelling of moth balls. I carried them out to the back porch and spread the clothes out to get rid of the smell. Normaine could have them after they aired out.

I tackled the third box. It was packed full of a lethal shade of pink organza resembling frothy Pepto Bismol. The stuff expanded as soon as I opened the box. I stood over the giant mound of pink stuff sticking up out of the box, growing larger every second, searching for inspiration. Now that I was an artist, I knew I could reclaim anything. What to do with the pink, frothy mountain growing steadily out of its cardboard box? I remembered watching those blob movies back in Ardenville. Would the pink blob take over the store, gobbling up all the Twinkies in its wake?

Inspiration struck me. Mama liked to sew. And she was good at it. I packed as much of the dreadful pink stuff back into the box as I could and dragged it into the back where Mama still sat on the Hideous Green Sofa, staring off into space. I wished she'd give up on hoping to visit aliens, but no, that wasn't in her nature. I thumped the box down in front of her.

"Mama, I know you like to sew. Here. Make something out of this."

She peered up at me. Then she looked at the Pepto Bismol pink foamy organza. I waited while she thought it over. I wasn't going to move until she did, if it took forever. She looked at me like she knew what I was thinking, and finally stabbed the air with one word.

"Tutus?"

Whatever she decided to make was fine with me.

"Fine. Whatever," I nodded and ran out back to the Merc' to find her sewing things before she drifted back into a coma.

And so it came to pass that Mama began making tutus. When the clothes on the back porch stopped stinking of mothballs, I packed them back into the cardboard boxes and set them aside for Normaine to make rag rugs out of.

Chapter Five

"I loves ya' baby, ya' skinny bony ankles an' yo' silk
dress,
doan' do me bad, promise ya'
daince' wid' only me, me, me, 'til's
we hangs up our daincin' shoes
plumb wore out and holy agin'
from Miss Minnie's saingin' of da' blues
When it's time ta' rest."

It took me awhile, but I finally got past Ray's
beauty and we made best friends. He taught me how
to make armpit farts and to spit. Soon he was better
than me on the armpit farts, but I could spit father
than he could. We went for long walks in the desert. I
searched for bugs and lizards while Ray examined
the colors and textures of the desert.

Ray liked to dig holes. I didn't care. I just strolled
in circles around him while he excavated, digging like
a dog with sand flying in the air. I made my circles
around him big enough to not get hit by the sand. I
spent a lot of time thinking up good questions to ask
him because he would answer anything honestly
when he was digging. I wanted to see who he was
without his usual guarded, beautiful outer trappings.

"You're a Measurer, Ray, aren't you?"

"What do you mean?"

"You like to dig down and know with a capital K
instead of staying on the surface and letting that be
enough."

"I guess so. Hell, I don't know yet. I'm too young. So are you. Stop asking stupid questions when I'm about to discover a new layer of human existence never revealed before."

He stopped and grinned at me each time he scolded me, and I always gave in. After all, he was an older man. I was already developing the habit of assigning him power and attributes he didn't have and never would.

Back at the store, Cowboy Johnson, Ray, and William the Dude took to roaming around like a herd of lost cattle. Wherever the women weren't, there they lit and stayed, bonding and doing manly things like spitting, guffawing really loud and drinking beer. In between customers, of course. Sometimes the customers joined them. I thought it was funny. One day I minced up to them and smiled.

"Afraid of us little ol' gals?" I asked, batting my eyes.

"Nah! We're just giving ourselves room to breathe! You ladies are a little too industrious for us laid back gentlemen!" William the Dude answered.

"I'm afraid of them!" Ray laughed and admitted.

I put my hands on my hips.

"Well, you shouldn't be! We're just two zombies and a kid!"

"Sounds like you've stood enough. Have a soda with us, kid?" William the Dude offered.

"No, but I'll have a beer," I challenged.

They all looked at each other, and I gave them credit. None of them said a word or cracked a hint of a smile. I felt like crying.

"Okay," William the Dude agreed.

Love just engages. It does not explain itself to anyone. They met me where I was. It was better than me crying all over them. I drank my beer and studied these three men. All three of them were friends of mine now. My heart lifted. I didn't feel like crying any more. What sparked the caring that grew between us? What was the spiritual purpose of love, honesty and Goodness? I didn't know, but these guys had it. I just wished Mama would stop fighting with the Universe and enjoy life for a change. It was the Boss, she wasn't. And it was fun too. Mostly.

I finished my beer, burped loudly, and said to them, "Did you know that the stinky stuff inside desert beetle guts make up approximately sixteen percent of their body weight? That they thrive on the banks of the Suez Canal? Nobody knows how they got there. Beetle Roadies. I suspect it may have been on the backs of half dead, worn out pack mules... or braying, ornery, biting, long toothed donkeys...Maybe they like the smell of rotted water beetles too. What do you think?"

They backed up, shrugged, rolled their eyes at each other, and walked off together. So much for enjoying the closeness of the moment.

*

Then Eddy showed up one morning while Normaine was organizing yet another wind chime. She didn't make them, she built them, then organized them. Her jilted, ex–betrothed–sweetheart–lover–boyfriend showed up at the store in Esmerelda, towing a long silver trailer that looked like a giant silver toaster. Riding with him were his three sisters,

Algestine, Aleda, and Alena. Cowboy Johnson and I hosted a long, drawn out mid-morning feast on the front porch for Eddy and his three sisters while they waited for Normaine to make up her mind whether to take him back or not. She took him back, and the silver trailer got parked out by Normaine's little pink trailer.

Thus began what Cowboy Johnson dubbed as the latest store and gas station soap opera, "Nights of Pink Trailer Love."

The three sisters stayed in the silver trailer. Eddy slept here and there, warding off his disapproving sisters until they were asleep so he could sneak out to Normaine's little trailer. His sisters never knew where he was going to sleep, though they asked him countless times each day.

"On Cowboy Johnson's extra air mattress."

"In Esmerelda. She needs the company"

"Out by the campfire."

"Out in the desert so I can be alone."

"Under the tree because it's the only one around."

"Down the road so I can watch the stars."

"In the store so I can guard the vegetables."

Since we were in a desert which didn't have any trees, and there were no other buildings around for miles, and the vegetables didn't have feet, they were having a hard time hiding their lust for each other. Finally, they took up staying nights in the garage at the side of the store on a rollaway camper cot they'd snuck in; one of several purchased when another beige outbuilding from Duke's Economy Readymade Shed was added up on the hill.

Eddy's three sisters knew what was going on. When Normaine and Eddy came out of the garage one morning, sleepy, happy, and tousled, they discovered his three sisters sitting in a row in rockers on the front porch, glaring at them. The two of them froze like deer caught in headlights.

Finally Eddy said, "Sure glad we finally got that carburetor cleaned, aren't you, Normaine?"

Eddy rolled his eyes over at her and yawned.

"Yep," was all she could manage, while she studied both the porch and the blacktop with one eye on each of them. Eddy took her hand and they pranced up the steps past his three glaring sisters who never spoke a word.

"Tonight, we got that truck to overhaul. Could take us all night again."

Eddy threw the words defiantly back over his shoulder at them.

"Yep," Normaine said.

The screen door slammed behind them. I watched Cowboy Johnson hastily go down the steps and rush around the side of the store. I followed him out of curiosity, and found him leaning against the back wall, laughing.

"Lord, help us!" he said, laughing some more. "We'll have to rename our soap opera "Dirty Carburetor Love," or "Nights of Forbidden Car Bay Love," or..."

When the three sisters weren't plaguing Eddy about his whereabouts, they spent their time rocking and knitting on the front porch, greeting customers, the milkman and the delivery guys, thoroughly evaluating the local crop of bachelors. By this time, Mama was calling them the Mafia sisters.

The Mafia sisters didn't have enough to do, which meant trouble brewing.

The trouble came quickly. They started making fruitcakes. Each fruitcake mixture needed to sit for three weeks before it could be baked, and some of them longer. The store was filled to bursting with smells of brewing yeast and alcohol emitting from the bowels of the bubbling containers stored everywhere.

After three weeks, they baked the first fruitcake in Cowboy Johnson's oven. They baked it Saturday morning. By the time I got home from my painting lesson with Miss Emma, all that was left was a tiny slice. The three sisters, Cowboy Johnson, Mama, Normaine, and Eddy were all very happy. Their faces were flushed, and they wore big grins.

"Here. We saved this for you."

They laughed and urged me to eat the tiny piece of fruitcake. I nibbled on it. It was okay. I was hungry, so it didn't matter that it was peculiar tasting. I ate it, and in about five minutes, my stomach felt hot inside. I started laughing.

"See?" The three sisters nodded approvingly.

"Drunken Fruitcake! We're going to make drunken fruitcakes and sell them. That's going to be their name!"

"Yeah!" I burped loudly and turned to Cowboy Johnson.

"Remember when I first met you?"

"Yes?"

"Well, I meant to tell you that the smelly, unified, grossly under rained, sparse, and skimpy juniper tree at the side of the store, besides needing watering it never gets but should, shame on you- if it's to top out correctly with a crown halo- it already has a halo around the top two branches and the halo is headed for the top of the tree if you will just keep it watered."

"Oh?"

I nodded happily.

"Yeah. It's more than halfway there. It is hanging out by your store because it's happy that your Goodness lives here. To it, you are a kind of Buddha."

The three hard core Catholic sisters sucked in their breaths and crossed themselves. I didn't care. I grinned at them. I felt happy. I even liked them for a change. I waved a hand at them.

"Oh, don't worry! It likes you three the best because you smell like black licorice," I explained magnanimously to them.

"Sorry, Cowboy Johnson, but you don't go around that side of the store very often, and they do. To get to the Silver Toaster," I explained.

And so, the Era of Fruitcake began. Pots, pans, and various containers filled every empty spot in the store. The sisters kept Cowboy Johnson's oven going all the time. The place smelled like a brewery and quickly filled up with happy customers.

Cowboy Johnson picked out a fruitcake every now and then, wrote his name on a piece of tape, stuck it on his Saran wrapped fruitcake, and kept it for himself.

William the Dude became a regular fruitcake customer. He ate some every day. Then he began sitting on the front porch with Algestine. Before long, he was a walking testimonial for her fruitcake. He said it was good for arthritis, lumbago, and whatever else ailed a body. He said it might even get you saved.

Soon the store and the front porch was filled with fruitcakes, painted lizards, snakes, bugs and birds, colorful rag rugs, and wind chimes. Wind chimes swung from long nails Normaine hammered into the rails and walls and of the front porch and wherever else she took a notion to hang one. Cowboy Johnson didn't complain. But he drew the line at hanging them on the back porch.

"The front porch is public. The back porch is private," he said in a tone that brooked no argument.

The wind chimes made all kinds of screeching sounds and weird noises when the wind blew, causing a few cars and one semi to swerve off the road, prompting a hasty trip to the local library by Cowboy Johnson and William the Dude to check out wind chime improvement books. There weren't any, so they drove to Albuquerque to find suggestions to tone down the raucous symphony of sound filling the store when the wind blew. They couldn't find anything except a book on chapel bells telling them the higher they were, the more perfect the sound.

But they underestimated Normaine. Just as they loved to tinker with old cars until they were perfectly tuned, Normaine tinkered with the wind chimes until they were perfectly tuned. She hung each one up somewhere and listened to its screeches, honks and bellows. After she knew its sounds, she took it down and hung it in front of a fan, turned the fan on, and adjusted the bits and pieces until each one sounded just right. She hunkered down and tapped and prodded with wire and pliers and cutters. Whenever she strapped on her carpenter belt with her tools in it, everybody went the other way—even Eddy.

After investigation and redistribution, the collective melodies of the wind chimes were nostalgic and sweet, except when a short, strong gust of stray wind rattled their organization into loud complaints and bitter melancholy for a few minutes.

Normaine said, "Ahh… they're like everything else. Gotta' bitch a little about life once in a while."

Pieces of tin and wires and bottle caps and slips of glass and nuts and bolts hanging and swinging together in the wind, made mellow music drawing in tourists who wanted to know who the artist was. When Normaine came out smiling, looking at them with one eye and at something else with the other eye, most of them hid their surprise. Artists were supposed to be eccentric, right? They expected that. They stayed and bought.

Normaine was gifted. Her work held a sophistication to it that came from her inner workings, not from her consciousness. We were artists, creating fruitcakes, rugs, wind chimes, lizards, bowls, and little clay people. We were on a roll! But there was big problem I needed to deal with before I could relax and be completely happy.

"Ray, want to go for a walk?"

By now he knew that this meant I wanted to talk something over with him.

"Sure."

He was the only one I didn't speak in smelly parables around. For whatever reason, my Sight never activated around him. It seemed to go on vacation when Ray was around. I called it "The Zen of Ray"—the altered state of being I went into whenever he was near. That's how beautiful he was. Of course, I never let him know that.

We ran out the back door and down the steps. I raced him to the remnants of last night's campfire and lost. We balanced ourselves on the logs, squaring the outer perimeters of the campfire area and walked them in circles. He waited for me to speak.

"Mama's getting better."

He nodded and stepped carefully to the next log, his arms out straight and wide for balance.

"That means she'll want to leave here. I don't want to. She's not good at taking care of us by herself. I have to help her. I'm the grown-up for both of us."

Ray said, "Well, I can give you a ride to school and back. And she can take over my job when we go back to school. How about that?"

"But will Cowboy Johnson let us stay here?"

Ray snorted.

"Duh! The way he obviously feels about you and your Mama? I think you could stay 'til doomsday and he wouldn't mind."

I jumped off the log I was walking and ran to Ray.

"Whoohoo!" I shouted and ran in circles around the campfire while he laughed.

"Owl Girl!" he shouted.

I gave her my speech when she started her speech about leaving. It was time for us to get on the road again, to search out a place to put down permanent roots, blah, blah. I set the clay lizard I was carving down on my work table and stared at her. She sounded like a spaceship officer preparing to blast off into unknown parts of the universe.

"No Mama. We're staying here."

"What do you mean? We've got to find a place and I have to get work before you start school again!"

I stared down at the table to keep from looking at her. She just didn't get it. We were already home.

"I've solved all those problems, Mama."

I knew she would be relieved. If only secretly.

"Cowboy Johnson said we could stay here as long as we like. He will change our names for us. Ray said he can pick me up for school and bring me home, and you can take over Ray's job because Cowboy Johnson needs the help."

I announced all this in one long breath.

Mama paced back and forth, reconciling the idea of the only child instead of the parent providing the solution as to how to live and provide, then going over the solution itself for flaws while the child waited.

"I'm not sure what to do," she protested weakly and sat down, trying to retain the last remnants of her power over my childhood. But she was no longer the boss. I was.

"It's okay Mama. Let's just do it this way for now. If it doesn't work out, we can change it later. And I want a middle name. And a new last name. I need it. I've earned it. I want it to be Athena. Geena Athena Johnson," I announced, looking her straight in the eyes. Then I added the big "P" word. For the first time ever.

"Please."

She looked at me for a long time. Then she got up and left. I kept on shaping the piece of clay into a lizard. I knew the answer. The plan would work because I said, "please," to her. I did it on purpose to soothe her pompous soul, who assumed it owned every other soul it liked, especially mine.

She came back in a few minutes and said, "Okay. But if I order you to do something without explaining it that's coming from my Sight, so you best do it! Got it?"

"Yes. Mama, I will."

She stomped off like a starship captain whose crew had finally mutinied. The changing of the guard was over. It was final. We could start over now. Mama tended to drag things out 'til doomsday, but I shrewdly nipped that unlovable tendency in the bud this time. Her agreeing with my plan would separate us in a new way and change forever the way we loved each other. It gave Mama guilt and me freedom. No more mother daughter routine that didn't work. For either of us. It was out in the open. A hell of a relief for me. That's the way it's always been with us. Everything changes. Even life and hope and love.

After I met Miss Emma, I changed again inside for some reason. I suspected she was her own version of Athena instead of Emma too. After all, her paintings could wipe out a regiment, a squad, a whatever- a plethora of meanness by shoving it straight into Awe using eyesight as its vehicle. Miss Emma's Sight was wired differently than Mama's. Miss Emma's was organized, sensible. All Mama did was hunt up the negative and worry about not being reliable because of her Sight, which she wasn't in some ways. She still believed Shadows were always huge. Not so. I knew at my age that some were small, sneaky little things.

"Why isn't Mama like you?" I asked her.

"What do you mean?"

"Well, you have the Sight, too."

I watched Miss Emma's line run off the paper she was drawing on. She didn't look up. I handed her a clean sheet of paper.

"But Mama always looks for the scary stuff, the bad stuff, and you look for the good stuff."

She said, "It's not "looking for" dear, it's what we see. There is a big difference. We see what we see, good or bad. It's given to some to see more bad than good."

"No choice?"

"None."

She looked me square in the eye then instead of away as she usually did with people.

"And you will do well to remember she is not weak, just gifted in areas you are not. Maybe her strengths have not been called out yet. Maybe until they are, she will be perceived as weak. Who knows? After all, we none know what strengths we have or how strong they are until we are called upon to unleash them for the greater good of all. And, the more they are used, the stronger they become."

I stared at tiny, immaculate, beautiful Miss Emma.

"And remember, all three of us have the gifts of my father, Ray, and Avery Mott Judson in our lives."

She didn't say any more. Neither did I. She stayed quiet and sent me home early. Ray drove me home.

"Did you know Cowboy Johnson's name is Avery Mott Judson?"

"Mom told you?"

I nodded with excitement. I couldn't wait to tell Mama!

Ray said, "It's supposed to be a secret! You better not tell anyone his name, either! Especially after all he has done for you and your Mama!"

"Why not, Ray?"

He looked at me like I was a true walking zombie moron.

"Because he doesn't want his family to find out where he is!"

I sighed and looked at Ray. A long silence followed. I said, "We don't want my father or our family to find us either."

"Why not?"

I searched for a way to answer him. After a minute I found it.

"My father likes me too much, and our families don't like us enough."

I could feel my face burning. Ray looked at me. I could see the wheels turning.

"Too much?"

I nodded, not trusting myself to speak. And waited. Finally, he said, "Oh. I get it...I'm glad you got away."

We rode in silence the rest of the way to the store. When I got out, I said, "I will keep Cowboy Johnson's secret and I need you to keep my secret too, Ray."

"I will." He drove away, late for his ranch chores.

*

The store was becoming more popular so we stayed open extra hours. We were all having the time of our lives. Us desert rats-misfits- were being accepted and validated by other people. That's when Cowboy Johnson and William the Dude decided to build a motel.

"Too many people in the store," Cowboy Johnson complained.

"People milling around like a herd of cattle. Gets so crowded I can't walk through here."

William the Dude laughed.

"Bet we could fill a motel with this big crowd."

I watched the two of them stare at each other like a light bulb just came on. Or exploded. Or blew out.

"Well, why not?" Cowboy Johnson pushed his dark green cap with the duck logo on it farther back on his head. They took off together while I went back to tending to my wares. They added a gift shop, a restaurant and extra rooms each for Mama and me and the Mafia sisters.

This was my permanent home. My room was big and clean and new. Now I could put down roots. If Mama ever left, she would leave on her own, without me. My place was here. It was mine with or without her.

Each one of us misfits were taking chances on our secrets being discovered by settling in one place. We were isolates of our species, desert rats, creative pioneers. The desert kept us safe, surrounding us with an ocean of sand and heat and nothingness— things most people didn't want anything to do with. It was an unwanted patch of land for unwanted people dwellers.

Naturally, we picked up on each other's negative residues faster than a speeding bullet. We all recognized each other's miseries the instant we met. Us misfits knew about walking in other's shoes, so to speak, so any emotional content laying around was subject to our scrutiny.

Intelligent, sensitive, allergy ridden, we were loaded with suspicions, hunches and feelings about each other and everyone else, almost always accurate. We never talked about most of our quirks or the Shadows following us through life. We just acted accordingly, helping each other out, and a few others passing through. We shared a low threshold of endurance for loud sounds and too much fake light and smell, so we needed the great, hot, empty outdoors we were stuck in. It seemed to need us, too. We were cantankerous, moody, dreamed-filled nomads waxing ecstatic over nightly campfires in a hot desert. Normaine said that was because of the hot dogs and moon pies.

And so, the motel building began. We reasoned we could feed people, then they could rest up in one of the eight motel rooms filled with colorful rag rugs, unusual looking lizards, and of course, complimentary fruitcake along with its results, snow white sheets on soft beds, and pull down window shades to block out the sun at nap time.

Who cared about ragweed outside the back door, or that there were outdoor johns and showers when there were deep shaded porches in bright, soothing watercolors, with comfortable rockers loaded with soft shawls and pillows in front of each room, shaded back stoops with bordered paths of white painted rocks and light strings of dancing, laughing hula girls, red peppers, blue crabs, and Christmas lights leading the way at night to their private outhouse?

Cowboy Johnson built a garden chapel for Mama. I took it over and filled it with clay lizards and pottery. Mama added flowers and vegetables Normaine added wind chimes. It became a short, bracing, suck it up scenic tour for whoever's spirit needed a break.

Customers ate pasta in the restaurant. They bought lizards, rugs, crosses, and fruitcakes in the gift shop. Cowboy Johnson put four ovens in the restaurant. He said they were for baking the Mafia sister's fruitcakes.

"It was self-defense. The store smells like a bar and customers keep asking for margaritas instead of soap or bread. I was forced to do it."

There were so many customers, we turned the extras away. None of us felt victimized by life any more. Together, we were healing ourselves, and our combined love filled up the store, spilled over, and sometimes surprised customers benefitted from the overflow.

Discretion being the better part of valor, the healing work we were called on to do for customers was disguised as customer service, clumsiness, samples of free fruitcake, and in several cases, identity theft.

"Oh, I'm sorry I hugged you so hard! I thought you were my nephew from Omaha!" this said to a seven-year-old boy with a walker who sat on the porch listening to the wind chimes while his parents went in the store to pay for gas and buy the boy a cold orange Nehi. His bones sounded like popcorn popping when I hugged him. I felt the straightening. The wind blew through the wind chimes to hide the sound. I knew the boy would get better now. The boy studied me as fresh color flooded his pale face. New energy lit his eyes.

"Thanks, lady!"

I stood up and moved away and watched as his doting parents came out of the store. They handed the boy his Nehi orange soda. I watched the sweat trickle down the bottle. He took a deep drink and handed the bottle back to them and stood up. He grabbed his walker and went down the porch by himself. They followed him with stunned looks. He stared back at me through the back window of their 1950 Ford Country Squire as they drove away.

We didn't put up a revival tent and advertise.

"Come All Ye Sinners! Preacher Lambastingus Healing Souls Under the Big Top Tonight!" But Martha found us anyway. We never knew her last name. And we never met another like her that needed our help. Thank God!

Mama and I were sitting on the front porch about three in the afternoon. We watched a woman in a rusty, tan station wagon with fake wood door panels stop in front of the gas pumps. She shut the engine off. The car shuddered to a stop. She stared up at us, the white bandage wrapped around her head making her look like an escapee from a mental ward somewhere. Mama and I stared at each other. I gave up first. She was mine. I sighed.

The woman opened her door and climbed out of the old station wagon, still staring at us. She made her way to the front of the station wagon so we could see her. She wore a plaid cheerleader's skirt, much too young and short for her, a tight white blouse stretched over large breasts and argyle red and white knee socks. A thick cloud of dirty red hair haloed her head. It looked like it hadn't been combed in months. Slashed across her mouth was a perfectly straight, heavy line of bright red lipstick, like a clown might wear.

"When I bent over to pour water in the cat's dish, the welcome mat on the floor inside the front door jerked itself out from under my feet. I grabbed for the doorknob, but it evaded me by flying open and hitting me on the head."

She threw her explanation at us in a whiny, throaty voice. We stared back at her and didn't answer. I bet she'd seen this reaction before. We wanted to laugh so bad it hurt, but we didn't want to be cruel, so we stayed silent in front of the macabre apparition addressing itself to us.

"I'm Martha," she said, and in slow motion, turned, groped along the battered fender and got in her vehicle. She waited until Cowboy Johnson finished gassing up her station wagon, paid him, and drove off.

He watched her car disappear into the distance and shook his head. There was nothing to say. We put the odd visitor out of our minds and forgot about her. We assumed we would never see her again, but we were wrong.

She showed up the next week at exactly the same time, as though she'd made an official standing appointment with us. Nobody was on the front porch. Cowboy Johnson rounded up Mama and me.

"Martha's back. She says she wants to tell you something."

"Who?"

"That weird lady."

We followed him to the front porch and sat down in rockers. Cowboy Johnson went down the steps and gassed up her car and ambled off into his newly expanded garage equipped with the latest hydraulic lift, leaving us holding the bag. I glared at his retreating back in disapproval. He was neglecting us lately in favor of spending his time in his fancy expanded garage equipped with all kinds of fancy new tools. He needed a good talking to.

After he disappeared, I focused on Martha again. She looked the same. The same slash of straight red lipstick, same clothes and giant mop of red hair needing tending and taming, the same bandage wound around her head. I watched her climb out of her beat up old station wagon and make her way carefully to the front of it again. By this time, Normaine was on the porch with us.

Martha rounded the front of the car and held up her left hand. It was bandaged, her left hand wrapped around a board, held in place with white gauze, her second finger sticking straight up in the air. I smothered a giggle. She was giving the world the finger! Ha ha!

"Heyoka!" Normaine whispered. She covered her mouth with the back of her hand and snickered fearfully. I didn't dare glance at Mama. We would have both burst out laughing.

"I was opening my front door, but it stuck, so I put this finger in the opening..." she waggled her second finger in the air, giving us the finger. "I thought it was the right size to push the door open, but it was too big and got stuck and swelled up and broke. The door wouldn't let go of it for a couple of minutes," she explained in her whiny, raspy voice.

Suddenly Mama jumped up and ran into the store with Normaine right on her heels. I glared at their retreating backs. I was left holding the bag. Again. I sat perfectly still, frozen in my endeavor to not laugh, watching Martha slowly give up.

She climbed back in her station wagon in, paid Cowboy Johnson, and drove away. Cowboy Johnson looked at me and shrugged. When she was out of sight, Normaine and Mama came back out on the porch. We all laughed guiltily.

The next week, Martha showed up right on time. The word had spread. Eddy, Normaine, Mama, Cowboy Johnson, William the Dude, Ray, and I were waiting on the front porch. She stopped in front of the gas pumps. Cowboy Johnson ambled down the steps to fill her gas tank.

The bandage around her head was gone. I felt relief. It was over. All of her explanations involved doors somehow. Maybe the concussion from a door somewhere was over. Red hair filled the driver's side of the station wagon, floating around like the pink organza Mama made tutus out of.

Martha fought her way out of the driver's seat and limped slowly to the front of the station wagon again. Her clothes looked exactly the same except for the too small red blazer she wore over the tight white blouse. I got the idea that she thought she was formally dressed when she wore it. I got the idea, instead of really knowing, because my Sight went on vacation every time she showed up. It ran off screaming, holding up a sign bearing the words, "Unwanted cousin! Beware!" for me to figure out.

Her second finger was still bandaged to the same board, stiff and sticking straight up, still giving the world the faithful finger, but now the ankle opposite her hand was heavily bandaged too, making her lean sideways and limp while giving it to the world. She ignored the snorts of suppressed surprise and titters from the crowd on the porch and directed her explanation to me.

"Two dog bowls and a welcome mat jammed themselves under the back door, and when I tried to pull them out, I caught my foot between the door and the jamb, and they twisted my ankle."

She waited for my response while standing on tilt with her bandaged handheld high in the air giving the finger to all and sundry. Thank God she didn't have the head bandage on too I thought.

The bunch gathered on the porch moved collectively and swiftly into the store while she stared at me. I stayed frozen in my rocking chair. I heard their smothered laughter. I hoped they were happy. I was left holding the bag again, and I didn't have a clue what to do with this weird looking, accident-prone, red-haired, weirdly dressed woman, who kept fighting with doors and rugs and whatever else and losing. There was no doubt she was losing. I'm sure it was painful. It looked it. It took all I could do to keep from laughing.

We stared at each other. She waited, but I was not further inspired. Nothing past guilty sympathy and the overwhelming need to laugh at her. She limped back down the side of the car, got in, paid Cowboy Johnson and drove away.

Okay. It was past time to pull myself together and stop laughing, at least internally, every time I saw Martha. I could control myself until she opened her mouth. But the combination of her looks and explanations was lethal to my sense of humor. I felt an impending sense of doom. I went inside and glared at the bunch gathered in the store. They snickered guiltily. My Sight felt guilty too. Good. It should. Maybe they all would straighten up now.

"Anyone know what the hell's going on?" I asked anyone in general.

"Heyoka!" Normaine answered. "The mask wearers. The Trickster has come to be healed. They always do it backward. They make you feel really bad for laughing at them instead of feeling pity for their predicament. They are elusive, and though they want to be healed, they will hide from you. Heyoka Shamans are rarely healed. They get old and bitter and blame all others for their pain because they are so clever."

"So, what do I do about it?"

Nobody knew. Normaine said nobody ever knew.

"Well, hell, I guess that fixes that!" I said bitterly and stalked off.

Two more gallows humor, guilt ridden Saturday encounters with Martha passed without anyone receiving a smidgen of inspiration about what was needed. The sixth Saturday rolled around. I sat frozen on the front porch in a rocker, waiting, a leaden feeling in the pit of my stomach. No donuts for me this morning. There was a pall over the store the last three weeks. Everyone felt guilty about Martha, so nobody ran away or hid like we all wanted to. We sat lined up in a row on the porch, waiting. Except for Cowboy Johnson, who couldn't stay away from his new garage gadgets. I glared at the garage resentfully. Yes, he definitely was in for a good scolding. If Mama wanted to spank him, she could after I was done scolding him. I thought about those things sometimes.

Sure enough, Martha drove in, right on time. Dismally, I waited for the usual scenario to take place, but Cowboy Johnson ran out of the garage, raised the hood of her car, propped it up, jerked out the dipstick and examined it. He shoved it back in, then slammed the hood down.

"You need an oil change," he shouted at her. She stared at him, then slowly, nodded.

"Drive into the car bay. Then go set up on the porch with Geena while I change the oil," he ordered.

She drove the station wagon into the bay. Cowboy Johnson ambled past and winked at me. I got it. And here I thought he was just drumming up an excuse to use his new hydraulic lift. Nope. He was trying an intervention.

He strolled past the passenger side of the station wagon and out of sight. I heard the new hydraulic lift purring smoothly, lifting the station wagon up so Cowboy Johnson could get under it easily to change the oil.

I waited on the porch for Martha, but she didn't come out of the garage. I got up and walked down the steps and into the garage just in time to watch Martha open the driver's door of the old station wagon which happened to be six feet up in the air. She stepped out and landed on the concrete floor. I made it to her before Cowboy Johnson ran around the other side of the rusty old station wagon.

"Christ! I thought she was up on the porch with you!" he said.

"I was looking for something in my purse. I keep my purse on the floor on front passenger side," Martha explained with a groan.

"Oh."

Light dawned on him.

"So, I didn't see you when I put the car up on the lift because you were bent over your purse on the passenger floor? Well, I'll be damned."

Mama appeared by me and grabbed my arm in a hard, demanding grip.

"Come on Geena! Go after your Sight! Make it come back! We have to strike while the iron's hot! Don't let your Sight get overwhelmed one more minute by Martha's spiritual inclinations! This was no accident! All of her bones are shook up enough from the fall-they're ready to prosper by new placement and release! But it has to be done right now! We've only got a few minutes!"

She grabbed Martha's legs and began to straighten her body out. I felt my Sight return. Suddenly, I was flooded with sureness—with knowing.

This being was a Heyoka Shaman. A Priestess. Royalty. She wore a mask to every healing, even her own. She needed to cross a threshold but kept getting stuck in the doorway. She was stuck because her ancestors, the genetics of which we all carry in our bones, were confused because Martha was a Trickster this lifetime. They didn't know whether to go or stay, so they bumped into each other every time she tried to cross any threshold, which many times, involved actual doors. They were confused and causing Martha's weird accidents.

"Wow!" I said under my breath. Now I understood.

"Work with her bones, Geena!" Mama urged. "Hurry!"

I touched Martha. Compassion filled me. A long, hard life. I saw her totem deer running around upside down in the underworld, their faces painted with rouge, lipstick on, long, false eyelashes loaded with mascara. They shoved their faces closed to mine, blew noisy kisses at me and whinnied like horses laughing before they ran away.

Cowboy Johnson knelt and held Martha up in his arms so I could reach her spine. I worked on touching each bone, releasing the messages and histories each one held, allowing it to reorganize.

Mama left and came back with Eddy and Normaine. Normaine smudged Martha with sweet grass and laughed at her, the proper Heyoka thing to do. Eddy poured baby oil over her wild red hair, rubbed the dirt out with clean garage rags, smoothed it down, and braided it. He left and came back with a red and black striped blanket. We laid her on it. She lay perfectly still, watching us, letting us do what we would. I glanced at Eddy and noted his ease with this situation and understood more. He'd tamed a wild woman before. Normaine was his wild woman; always would be.

Cowboy Johnson sat Martha up. I sent Normaine for my makeup and my little red transistor radio. She brought them back. I turned on the music and ordered the men to paint us and then themselves. When they finished, we looked like Martha always looked. We laughed at each other, and Martha joined in.

She belonged to her mirrored, backwards Way and was relieved to be seen and accepted by the mirrors. Those being us. She began talking, burping, and farting. Out poured old bursts of her ancient, internal people's words. The deer danced around her, laughing and farting too. With the words and burps came stenches, vapors, odors, and a variety of musty, pungent, putrid, rotten, and rancid smells. We jumped up and staggered around to get away from them, but we couldn't go far. We were bound by spirit to stay until this thing was through. Good thing the garage doors were open.

The burps and gas finally stopped. She fell into a doze, steeped in an altered space, gathering her strength back through sleep.

"Better lower the station wagon," I said to Cowboy Johnson. She was, after all, a Shaman Heyoka, which made her do the opposite, so she might be in a rage when she woke up and pour hate out on us instead of love.

The others slipped out. I sat with her and waited until I saw the flush of pink suffuse her cheeks as she came back into herself. By that time, I had moved to safety.

Sure enough, she sat up, glared at me balefully, and shouted in an old man's voice. "By God, you've done it now! You've ruined me!"

She pulled herself up from the floor and shambled awkwardly to the station wagon now parked outside. She climbed in and tore off, tires squealing, cursing us, pointing her taped up second finger at us.

Normaine laughed.

"We did good!" she crowed.

"We did?"

"Yes, dumbasses! She's Heyoka! She's doing just the opposite of what is expected. That's all. The Trickster has been healed!"

We never saw Martha again, Thank God! But six months later, we received a post card from Peru signed- Evelyn H. (you know what for) Smith. On the postcard was a picture of a bunch of native people sitting in an adoring circle around a fuzzy red-headed Shaman with her back to us.

Ĉhapter Six

I was never strong enough to make ya' not stray,
Ya' purty thaing, you,
yep... yep...yep...
Hell, I was barely strong enough
to make ya' stay as long as ya' did.
Yep ..yep...yep..

"Babe, have you seen my razor?"

I looked at Ray in the mirror. He was as beautiful as the first time I laid eyes on him.

"No, I haven't. Maybe it's in your overnight bag."

He looked at me and grinned.

"What's in your overnight bag?"

I blushed and tried to act sophisticated. Ray and I and a bunch of friends were spending the night in two of the motel rooms. I bought the skimpiest nightgown I could get away for the occasion while Mama stood over me. I pulled it out of my bag. It was ankle length, made of white cotton, but at least it didn't have long sleeves like Mama wanted.

"Girls in room one. Boys in room eight. I'll be supervising," Mama stated grimly. Ray was in college, and I was in love with him as much as ever. There was just a moment in the motel room to pretend we were an old married couple.

"What are the kids doing?"

I batted my eyes at him and giggled.

"They are at the babysitters, little heathens!"

"They take after you, honey," Ray said. He ran a slow finger up my arm. Ray already knew I never wanted kids. We had talked about it and he didn't either. We were just playing.

Mama spent a lot of time seeing to it that our romantic moments were few and far between. Ray pulled me into his arms, and we necked hastily before our friends poured into the room laughing and shouting, their hands filled with sodas and munchies from the store. It was time to celebrate the motel being finished with a pajama party.

After the motel was finished, we moved into our rooms. I painted mine pink and green and filled it with collections of bugs and ants and plants. Mama's room looked like she'd joined a monastery or planned to live out of a suitcase forever. She kept the Merc' parked right outside her door.

The Mafia sisters shared a small sitting room, empty except for one short, rock-hard sofa. End tables and a coffee table surrounded it. On the walls by the windows hung crosses and black velvet pictures of Jesus looking soulful and greatly in need of a haircut.

But their bedrooms were another story. Each one held a high, vast acre of bed, standing proudly in the middle of the bedroom. Tall, ornate, dark headboards swept the ceilings while dark ornate footboards held the bed's length at bay. Matching dressers hugged the wall like solemn, dark soldiers. Long, oval mirrors on stands and night tables encased in more dark wood stood beside of the ornate beds. But that's where the likeness ended.

Aleda's huge bed was swathed in layers of purple bouffant and piled high with huge white pillows, candy boxes, lilac throw pillows, and purple shawls. Round night tables stood on each side of her bed. Purple scarves reclined across the lamp on their tops, giving the room a sullen purple glow when the lamps were lit. A wood radio shaped like an arched window ruled the top of her dresser. Her closet was next to the dresser. It was filled with clothes, shoes, hats, and stacks of shawls and scarves. Above her bed was an ornate silver cross with a weary Jesus hanging on it.

Alena's bedroom was painted the same sedate green as the sitting room. Her high, vast bed was covered with crisp, snow white sheets and pillows, with a folded green blanket at the foot of the bed. Her lamps stood austere and tall, thin and shiny and pale green, in the middle of the white lace doilies centered perfectly on her night stands. A rocker sat near the window so she could have more light to read her Bible by. The cross above her bed was plain, simple wood without Jesus occupying it.

While everybody was settling into their rooms, Normaine and Eddy moved into motel room number five.

"It's next to the sanctuary," Normaine explained to his sisters.

Eddy rolled his eyes at them innocently.

"Yeah. We have twin beds with night stands in between so we can snack and talk all night. We wanted to be nearer the chapel so we can visit it all the time."

After they moved in, Cowboy Johnson renamed the store's soap opera "Room Number Five's Twin Beds of Love."

We knew they would leave us in time. We didn't know when or how. Just that the time would come, and we would have to accept it. Normaine was a Great Plains Indian. Her ancestry was nomadic. It was genetic with her. And Eddy liked being on the move.

"But not on the lam," he said, laughing. He began with tricycles, then bicycles and horses before he graduated to motorcycles and cars.

"When I started driving the big rigs, I knew I'd found my home," he said, dark eyes flashing, elegant, strong hands moving in bold gestures. Normaine always sighed and looked at him like he was the second coming of Christ, Elvis, and Tony Bennett rolled into one.

*

Christmas vacation wasn't far away by the time we all were settled in. I was in high school, my grades were good, and I made friends easily. This Christmas was going to be more special than usual because William the Dude was getting married to Algestine Savingo, the eldest Mafia sister.

I didn't know if I liked that or not, but maybe I was too young to understand the ways of grown-up love. Ray and I watched the high handed Savingo sisters ordering William the Dude around until he was worn out from it. We discussed it and neither one of us liked what was going on.

"Personally, I think the three Mafia sisters are too nutty about religion, don't you Ray?"

"Yep..."

"I'm afraid for grandfather," he said soberly.

"Why?"

"He's having a hard time with all the rules put on him by the sisters. I know he's a patient man, but I hate to see him lassoed and hog tied like a goat and hauled off to the slaughter of his manhood. That damn fruitcake has him blinded to it."

I stared at him, open mouthed.

"A goat?"

He didn't laugh.

"You know what I mean. He won't have himself anymore. And he's old. She'll ruin who he is."

"Fruitcake?"

"Yep. They should call them booze cakes."

Light dawned on me. Wow! I sure didn't put two and together on that one!

"So, William the Dude is addicted to fruitcake?"

Ray nodded. "To HER fruitcake. Algestine."

We watched William the Dude patiently negotiate his love with his intended. He never won. She always won. An arrogant triumph on her part not giving us cause to like her better. Then one day, William the Dude couldn't take it anymore. He collapsed on the front porch and Cowboy Johnson and I loaded him into Esmerelda and took him to the little hospital in Pistachio Pico.

Anyway, I sat in that little waiting room thinking about God and religion, wondering how much difference a fruitcake could make. The fruitcake took William's pain away. I guess that was what he really gave a damn about. Maybe there is a higher reason for each of us being exactly the way we are, and we should stop trying to be somebody else and eat fruitcake if that's what it takes to make us happy.

Walking the campfire logs last night I asked Ray, "They don't want him to get away, do they?"

He said, "Nope, they don't. He's already told her if it's an act she's putting on, he's leaving. She's finally signed a prenuptial agreement."

"What's that?"

"A legal agreement saying all he owned before he met her will stay his if they split up. She agreed not to protest legally if he ever wants to leave. He's done the same for her. He will provide her a generous pension, enough to live well on, if they ever break up. He said the prenup is as close as he can get to keeping the freedom he needs and still be married. He said he's glad he got sick and realized what her damned religion was doing to both of them. He still doesn't think the fruitcake is a problem or the reason he is marrying her."

Ray grabbed me and hugged me. I leaned back in his arms and looked at him.

"So, if you're going to be rich someday, Ray, and could have more than one vehicle, what would you buy?"

"No cars. Another truck. Maybe an orange truck with black pin striping and a few flames on the sides."

He smiled at me.

"What would you buy?"

"Maybe a Ford Thunderbird Supercharged! I can picture us making dust devils in it in Washman's Draw!"

Forgetting the cars, we kissed. And kissed some more.

*

William the Dude married Algestine on Christmas eve. There was a reception in Pistachio Pico before they left for Santa Fe. The next morning, everybody crowded into the store to celebrate Christmas day. The Mafia sisters were still wearing their beige and purple outfits. They solemnly baked a ham in Cowboy Johnson's oven. Cowboy Johnson brought in a big red bag of goofy Christmas presents for us. I got a pink boa, a paste tiara, and a rubber chicken, but the main thing I celebrated was not being in Ardenville for Christmas for the first time in my life. I cried and Cowboy Johnson, my good father, hugged me.

While we ate dinner, I tried to not think further than Christmas. Time would fly by too fast, causing Ray to leave us again. I knew from experience I would suffer until he came home. I planned our future though I never told him. I took it for granted we would spend our lives loving each other as man and wife when the time came right. Him or me loving someone else never entered my mind. We were made for each other. He was mine, part of my heart and soul.

But still, sometimes for an instant, I admitted to myself that he wasn't like me. There was a calculating, distant coldness about him that scared the hell out of me sometimes.

Vacation ended. Ray left for college. I went back to high school. He came home for a couple of weekends and things were fine. We went on as usual. Then he came home the third weekend from college and hesitated before we exchanged our usual enthusiastic hugs. I hugged him anyway, but he stared over my head and didn't smile at me.

Her name was Dinah, and she almost killed me, although I'm sure she never knew it. I didn't understand until he came right out and told me. He asked me to meet him out at the campfire, so I knew it was serious.

"Hey, kiddo. I've got something to tell you."

Ray never called me kiddo. I froze at his tone, stumbled and fell off the log I was walking. Hurt and angry, I tried to pick a fight to avoid the death I knew was coming.

"Who do you think you are, Ray? A big shot college boy now? Huh?"

He ignored my words.

I got up, caught completely off guard, swaying like I was caught helpless in a strong wind as he spoke. His words shattered my heart and dreams and life into a thousand little pieces. I heard and felt the sharp shards of them falling all around me. My heart's bones and blood shredded and fell away. In their place stood a newborn, shivering with shock, trying to just breathe and survive.

"Dinah. New in college. She's blond and just moved into town and she's in my classes."

He waited for an answer from me. There wasn't any. Would never have any for this.

"We're so young. We need to have other boyfriends and girlfriends so we can be sure if we want to be with each other."

Ray kept trying to talk himself into what he was doing. That's all I remember. I felt his arms go around me, but I couldn't lift mine to hug him back. He held me tight to him, ran his hands over my hair and face and held me tight to his body like he was memorizing me. Then he let go of me and walked away. I died and came back different in those moments, for I have never trusted a man completely like I did Ray when I was a girl, way back then, ever again. Some events change your life forever, and there is no going back, no matter how hard you try, what age you are, or what you believe in.

I sat down on a log. Somehow, it was my fault. I wasn't enough for him. Not pretty enough. Not smart enough. Used goods. My mind sank into darker and darker places. I thought about dying, and how easy it would be. Maybe I was like Mama and could die easy. After all, I was just told the worst thing I could ever hear.

Angry shouting interrupted my downward spiral. I never knew where my thoughts might have led me because all of a sudden Cowboy Johnson stood in front of me. Beside him stood Mama, her face white and angry. I wondered what was wrong, but I didn't know if I could ever speak again.

Cowboy Johnson swooped me up in his arms and carried me away from the campfire. He carried me up the steps and through the back door of the store with

Mama following. He set me down on the Hideous Green Sofa. Mama ran past him, grabbed me and held on.

It didn't help. Nothing would ever help that part of me killed by Ray's words. If he came in the door right now and took it all back, it couldn't unbreak what was broken. Mama spoke to Cowboy Johnson after a while.

"It's time for spaghetti. Would you fill the biggest pot you have with water and put it on to boil and check in the cupboards and see how much spaghetti and sauce you have?"

I kept my eyes closed and hid my face against Mama's shoulder. I didn't want to see the world ever again. I seemed to go in and out of reality. It felt like I slept, then I heard Normaine talking in a low voice with Cowboy Johnson about the spaghetti. The room filled with moist air and the smell of spaghetti noodles and sauce. I remembered all the times we ran away from home and got found. I started sobbing.

"This time, little one, he didn't find us and make us go back with him, remember? We made the spaghetti right here in Cowboy Johnson's store and we never went back to the bad man again," Mama said soothingly, running her hands over my hair. Normaine started crying at Mama's words. I felt her set down hard on the other side of me.

Finally, Mama said, "Some women never have to grow up in this way. They marry their childhood sweetheart, and all goes well, and both of them maintain unbroken hearts at all costs. They may hate each other eventually but won't risk the cost of the pain and learning that comes from enduring and mending a broken heart. Life will call you out and break your heart ever so often, that's a given, but many people turn from the pain of it. Life, death, love and loss. That's it."

I pulled my hair around me like a curtain and hid behind it.

"Spaghetti's ready," Cowboy Johnson announced. I stood up to get away from Normaine and Mama's embraces, wobbled over to the table and sat down. Cowboy Johnson slapped a ridiculously large plate of steaming spaghetti down in front of me.

"Reminds me of when we fed the three Mafia sisters on the front porch," he said dryly. I giggled in spite of myself.

*

Dinah moved away in about a month. Her family was military, and they moved on. After Dinah left college, Ray started trying to hang around me again. He came home for weekends and worked at the store. Cowboy Johnson left us to find our own way through the mess. We walked the logs at the campfire.

"Would you be out here trying to talk to me if Dinah was still in town? I think that's a damn good question, don't you?"

Ray stared at the ground, not saying anything.

"What are you gonna do the next time someone shows up you think is better than me?"

He still didn't say anything. Finally, he said, "You're all I think about."

"Liar! Get away from me! Don't come near me!"

I ran and ran and ran until I stood alone in the desert. My heart was pounding. My hair lay sodden against my head, glued to it with sweat. I slung my head back and forth. No! No! No! In deep anguish, I admitted what I already knew. There was no going back and pretending it never happened. We were changed. Who we were together was changed. Now we were me and him. Not us anymore.

I dragged myself home, back to my room. Ray's truck was gone. I sneaked into my room and lay down. Night came, and I lay there hour after hour, trying to let my life ebb away like I imagined Mama could do. But it didn't work.

I compared Mama and me in our thinking, and I admitted we were not cut from the same cloth. I didn't know what cloth I was cut from, but it wasn't hers or my father's. I was curious about life and tended to be happy go lucky. I saw the way to organize things very quickly. Normaine said I could be real bossy if I tried. I read everything I got my hands on, and I liked science and new ideas.

I asked myself a question. Instead of laying in the bed trying to be sad and dying over Ray, what was it I needed, instead of what Mama needed, to ease the pain I was stuck in? I waited, but I didn't get an answer.

"What time is it?" I muttered under my breath. I looked at the Big Ben clock on the nightstand. It was midnight. Only midnight? My body ached like I was chained to my bed. Damn, time went slow when a person was miserable!

I slipped out of bed, pulled on my jeans, a red sweater and tennis shoes, tied my hair back into a ponytail with a pink ribbon. I slipped out of my room, closing the door softly behind me. All the lights were out. Everyone was sleeping. Only a small light was coming from Cowboy Johnson's living quarters. He must be reading again.

I took a deep breath and looked around. The stars were shining in the sky. I was outside. In the world I loved. I took a deep breath and inhaled the desert smells. I looked up at the millions of stars in the black sky. I stood there waiting. I didn't know what I was going to do next, but it would be what was needed. At the ripe old age of seventeen, I trusted myself more than I trusted anyone else.

I wandered over to the campfire and walked the logs squaring its perimeter a couple of times. But it just reminded me of the many times Ray, and I walked them together and talked over our problems.

To hell with that! I decided I was hungry. I thought of starting a fire and roasting marshmallows. Bologna fried on a stick, cave man style, sounded great. I would just make a small fire and knock on the back door and ask Cowboy Johnson for some bologna.

I made the fire and hunkered down over it, waiting for it to grow. I heard a noise and looked toward the store just in time to see Cowboy Johnson framed in the soft light. He was shutting the door behind him. I watched him with mixed feelings as he walked down the steps and crossed the distance separating us.

"Mind if I join you?" he asked.

"I want bologna. Fried on a stick over the fire. And marshmallows. And maybe blueberry pie."

"You know where it's at. Get us a couple of Cokes, too okay? It's too late for beer."

He must have read my mind.

"Okay."

I returned with my arms full of food and two Cokes. I set them down on the old door laying across the top of tree stumps. We used it as a table. I handed him his Coke and sat down beside him. We stared into the fire and sighed. Then we looked up at the stars in the black night sky and sighed again.

"Sometimes life sucks," he stated.

I nodded.

It was a fact.

"Put the bologna on the stick for me," I ordered.

He nodded and picked up the stick and sighed again.

I wrinkled my nose at him.

"Why are you sighing? I thought it was just me that felt bad."

"Well, there's this story of an owl I was thinking about."

"What owl? Tell me the story."

"Maybe it's too sad for ya'."

"Do I look sad?"

I grinned. I didn't feel too bad. I folded a second thick sliced piece of bologna into quarters and speared it with a thin stick. I stuck it over the fire to fry and grinned again at him.

"This is the story of Damn Tom," he stated solemnly. "Well, there was once a great white owl that lived alone on the edge of this same desert. The owl's name was Damn Tom."

I snickered and turned the bologna over. It was sizzling, turning nice and brown and crispy.

"Sounds like somebody else is full of bologna, get it?"

Cowboy Johnson ignored my ignoble remark and went on with his story.

"Now Damn Tom, he was not your standard great white owl. He didn't know exactly what he was because he lived alone in the world. He'd named himself Damn Tom after he flew over the house he got water at one night, and heard a woman's voice calling out, "Damn Tom, where are you?

Houses out in the desert are far and few in between and at night they are generally closed up and dark. So Damn Tom searched out more houses and flew over them and found water, but he never heard any more voices calling out. So, he accepted the only inspiration that was sent to him, and he became content with his name. You see, he never met another owl. Just the bugs and mice and lizards he lived on and a road runner now and then. Damn Tom didn't know what it was to not be lonesome, but he couldn't figure out who to be lonesome for, because he didn't know anyone.

Now owls are wise. That's a given, so sooner or later, Damn Tom was bound to figure something out. Anything. He waited and waited. But time went on, and he didn't figure anything out. He just kept on sleeping under the lone mesquite tree growing in his part of the desert. He slept standing on the edge of a board that blew up into the mesquite tree during a sandstorm and stuck there.

Damn Tom perched on the edge of the board, watching the remnants of the skinny road running through the sand not far from the tree. He waited to see who would happen by. But nobody ever did.

He made a study of the road, and he drew conclusions. He knew the road would take him to other places if he traveled on it. But he didn't feel the urge to travel. Things weren't great, but they could be worse. So, he decided to pretend the road didn't exist. It was planned amnesia."

Cowboy Johnson stared into the fire for a while. I waited until a twig finally snapped, breaking his reverie.

"Damn Tom didn't know he wanted to avoid the heartbreak everything in life has to go through on the roads they choose to travel, no matter what creature, plant, or animal they are. Or mineral, or rock or saint. All he wanted to do was forget and stay just the way he was.

Well, it's true owls don't have many faults, just a few. But the few faults they have are mighty, and usually come from too much highbrow thinking or from solving too many advanced algebra problems in their heads.

But the biggest fault owls have is complacency. They become too content and don't want to leave their familiar territory when change comes knocking. Why, they will stay in a forest on fire and choke to death before they leave their nest! Damn Tom already was warned from past lives through dreams of his relatives holding their ground in a forest fire and ending up being roast owl because of their tenacity. He did not want that to happen to him, but it couldn't anyway, because he lived in a desert, and there were no trees, right? He had it all covered.

I nodded and ate my fried, crispy bologna while I watched Normaine and Eddy slip in and sit down on a log. My heart surged with love for them. And questions. I cocked my head to the side and stared at them. Eddy drove all the way from forever to come and find Normaine. I heard him say he would go to the ends of the Earth for her. How come Ray and I weren't like that with each other?

I once assumed all romantic love travels the same path for everybody. Boy, was I wrong! Oh, I knew hormones were a part of it. Chemistry. I assumed those things because everyone I knew was in love or married, laughed and looked at each other knowingly. I read meanings into those looks that might not be true. Maybe there was a part of true love for another that demanded seeing them as they were. Maybe some people settled for the pictures like I once did, and never looked behind them to see who was really there.

I wanted to cry. What about God? "God" was supposed to be living alone while running the show? What about Mary and Joseph and the rest of that bunch? Was God too Godly to be a part of a team or have any relatives? I heard He went in for team sports such as golf or bowling, but was "He" just a lonely jock like Ray might end up being? I shook my head to chase away the thoughts. I didn't want to grow up in this way! I looked away from Normaine and Eddy.

Cowboy Johnson was watching me, waiting to continue his story. I looked at him and nodded. He went on with his story while I tossed some more sticks on the fire. At least he would let me stay young. For a while. For tonight at least.

"Great white owls don't live in the desert, so how did Damn Tom get there? He often wondered. Sometimes mightily. Did somebody take him there under cover of dark and leave him? How did he know he was an owl? All he could go by was the half buried, busted metal cage lodged against the foot of the lone mesquite tree he lived in. All he remembered was flying through the air and hearing a voice yell "The owl!" just before the cage plowed to a stop under the mesquite tree. The cage door popped open and he crawled out of it, using his beak and talons. Then he climbed up in the tree and sat there, shaking his head.

He couldn't remember anything else. Did he have amnesia? Owl amnesia? Or maybe he was too young back then to remember. Damn Tom didn't know. He was stuck in the land of I don't know a damn thing, and what Damn Tom didn't know could fill a book. But his instincts served him well, and he was still able to hunt, eat, and sleep."

I watched Cowboy Johnson stop the story of "Damn Tom" for a minute while Mama sat down on a stump on the other side of the fire. I took the stick with the fried bologna on it from Cowboy Johnson and ate it. Then I speared more bologna on the stick and stuck it over the fire. Normaine was munching potato chips. Eddy was eating Twinkies and roasting hot dogs. Mama held a mug of tea in her hand. It was probably her favorite pink tea. Red raspberry. It made the most beautiful color when it was poured. Cowboy Johnson went on with his story.

"Now, Owl Knowing carries the Lunar wisdom of everything, but you have to search inside yourself if you want to ever find it. So, conditions forced Damn Tom to become even more of an introvert than owls usually were. He didn't feel like a kook or anything phony. He just felt like whatever he was, was something he didn't know much about yet, so he asked "Who?" a lot. But he got no answers.

Then one lonely, hot, summer day when Damn Tom was dozing under the shade provided by the board lodged in the mesquite tree, he heard a roaring noise. His large, round eyes flew open just as a large pink convertible fishtailed past him on the skimpy little road. The convertible threw up a plume of dust. The dust flew up into the mesquite tree and covered him. He heard voices laughing. Damn Tom flew down from the tree and coughed and shook and dived and soared until the dust was gone. He flew back into the mesquite tree again, landed on the board, and smoothed down his ruffled feathers.

Then he happened to look down. He saw a small round patch of blue at the bottom of the tree. Was it water? He was thirsty. He flew down under the tree and examined the hard, flat disc. A mirror lay up against the cage. It reflected the blue sky above the mesquite tree. Damn Tom felt his heart beat louder. He looked into the mirror, and at last, saw himself. He watched as he changed from a great white owl into a smaller owl with straight, long brown feathers and silly freckles around his beak. Where did he get the silly freckles from? Would he answer the call to adventure he felt? Where did the pink land yacht go? Were they having fun somewhere without him? Did they miss him?

Oh, maybe they knew things about him! After all, the mirror was from them. Maybe they were the owners of more things he could learn from! He needed to find them! He flew down the sandy myth of a road in the same direction as the pink convertible.

I smiled at Cowboy Johnson. How did he know Mama told me when I was kid that we were Owl Clan?

"Damn Tom flew so fast he caught up with the pink car and landed on the hood ornament. The people in the car were astounded by Damn Tom's beauty and vitality as he posed on the hood. They slowed down and drove really slow so he didn't get blown off of the hood. He went home with them, posed here and there on the hood and elsewhere, and slept in their den. They fed him his favorite foods, mostly dried mouse jerky, walnuts, pumpkin and squash seeds. They hoped that since Damn Tom was an owl, he would grace them with some of his wisdom. But being independent and an aged soul, like all owls are, Damn Tom, being an old soul in a young owl's body, did some reckoning. His hormones were roaring, and he blushed a lot. He visualized ice bergs to keep it down but living in a desert didn't help matters. He wanted a mate, then a family, but sensibly, a girlfriend should come first.

So, he flew away one day, and came back in a few days with a dainty little white owl named Lucky Coral. Lucky Coral and Damn Tom necked about for a while, but then Lucky Coral flew away.

Damn Tom figured she flew away because she was homesick, so he went to find her. To his dismay, he discovered Lucky Coral making a nest with another owl much bigger than him. Well, his heart broke into a million pieces. Damn Tom was jealous and mad, but he also retained his common sense. He flew back to his home, back to the people who relied upon his wisdom, and became a great white owl again.

For a long time, that's what he stayed, until a cute little brown barn owl named Lucy Charms flew by. She looked just like him! She batted her eyes at him, which made his feathers turn browner and his silly pink freckles to breakout all around his beak again.

He prepared to follow her, but the great white owl he once was had to stay behind, for Damn Tom would be a barn owl now. He didn't know where the barn was, but perhaps Lucy Charms could show him the way.

Damn Tom flew down and hastily gave his people some last words from the great white owl before he flew away. He advised them that The Way of the Heart was to be remembered. What it takes to mend a broken heart takes a different measure for each part of life. After life mends the heart, the ones involved in the heartbreak might become friends of a different sort and go through this world together. Or not. The great white owl told them, "That is the Way of the Heart. Never forget it."

Then Damn Tom said, "I'll be back." Which he knew may or not be a lie and flew away. Then he flew back and circled them. "Some day?" he added, for he knew that part was true, and he flew away.

Whooo? Did Damn Tom marry Lucy Charms and have charming little baby Tom Toms and Tomettes? Nobody knows, or ever will, until he returns. Maybe he is still out there waiting somewhere. That is all."

I watched Cowboy Johnson staring at Mama. I hoped she would return his look, but she didn't notice. Normaine got up and took Cowboy Johnson the hot dog she just finished turning black over the fire. She handed him the bun and asked, "Ketchup or mustard?" even though she knew he liked mustard and not ketchup.

"Dumbass!" I heard her whisper to Mama as she walked by her.

Mama dropped her head. I squinted at her, my mind filling with speculation. It didn't look like Mama knew any more about men at her age, than I did.

I felt better. I jumped up and danced around the fire. Normaine and Eddy jumped up too. They'd dance at the drop of a hat. I spread out my wings and hollered, "Whoo, Whoo? We're all Owl Clan!"

Then I began to warble, "Oh give me a home where the buffalo roam," at the top of my lungs. It was the only desert song I knew, and I wanted to tell the desert how much I appreciated it. Cowboy Johnson pulled Mama to her feet, held her hands, and led her sedately around the campfire in a sort of waltz, so I kept on singing.

Ćhapter Seven

Git' yourself in yonder baby,
go find you's some a dat' red lipstick
brush on some of dat' fine make up you owns
ya' knowed, sooner or later
wid' yo' fine, skinny, bony ankles,
ya'd hafta' learn a new tune
to keep ya' daincin."

Over time, I let Ray back into my life. Because I still loved him. "As a friend only!" I said, glaring at him. He nodded, eyes on the ground. We never walked the campfire logs and talked with the same freedom again. Prices have to be paid. But I was one who was by nature happy and curious about the world. I owned enough common sense for two people, so I checked out books from the library at Cowboy Johnson's suggestion, and read about teenagers like Ray and me. I read about boy's hormones raging and girls having to hide their strong feelings under a "gentle" exterior. Evidently, boys didn't like girls to have strong emotions.

Ray and I were once best friends. I once told him my secrets. My father never let me or Mama have any friends. Ray was my first best friend, then I fell in love with him. I thought the two worked together. But I was wrong. I needed girlfriends, so I began hanging out with Leeza, a girl in my class.

Leeza was brown haired, quiet, shy, a good student. She was poor. She wore the same clothes to school every day. A teacher gave her a winter coat to wear in the winter. She never brought lunch to school, so I started bringing extra and sharing with her. To help her save face, I complained.

"Look at this! Too much food in again! Geez! I don't want to get fat! You want some of this?"

I said this although I could eat half a beef and a whole pie in one sitting and never gain an ounce. I was taller and even more slender. I was in field and track and ran everywhere. But I was off my feed because I fell in love with Ray, then I was off my feed because of my broken my heart.

She couldn't afford all the textbooks we needed for our classes, so I kept an "extra" one she could borrow. We both understood what was going on. We never talked about it though. That was fine.

Leeza became my new best friend, someone to take Rays place. I invited her home with me and watched the way she was with Mama and Cowboy Johnson, and the rest of my beloved family. She thought they were "kind of different," but okay. I didn't have anyone over very often, for we all protected each other's privacy and ways. I let her think that we'd always lived at the store At last I knew to be cautious, to keep a part of me to myself, but the learning was costly and bitter.

I rode home with Leeza once on the school bus. That was enough. We sat on the front porch of the ratty house she lived in. The trees around the house were old and broken from her brothers climbing them, she said. They were full of bullet holes too, but I wisely didn't ask about that.

She was the oldest of four sisters and three brothers. Her sisters hid in the house and watched us from behind the curtains. They wouldn't come out and talk to us. Leeza's mother called us in to eat after forever passed.

There were no men or boys anywhere around. The place was deadly quiet like something bad was going to happen. I hastily ate the few soup beans out of the small bowl Leeza's mother handed me, with a smidgen of cornbread and a small glass of milk. That was it.

"Would you mind if I called for my ride now? I just remembered a bunch of chores I have to do."

Leeza's mother jerked her thumb toward the black dial phone hanging on the wall beside a tiny plastic wall clock. I looked at it. I looked at her. I didn't like her. I had been here exactly forty-five minutes. When Cowboy Johnson came to pick me up, I was damned glad to get the hell out of there.

"I need a car of my own," I complained, not for the first time. He nodded, not for the first time.

"Talk to your mother."

By the time we got home, I was loaded for bear. I stomped up the steps and across the porch. I flung the screen door wide open, stomped inside, and over to the counter where Mama was waiting on an elderly gentleman. I paced back and forth, glaring at them. They ignored me. I stepped it up. I drummed my fingers on the countertop and cleared my throat. They stopped their chit chat and the elderly man grabbed his fruitcake, quickly counted his change, and left. I launched into my tirade.

"Why can't you ever take me seriously, Mama? You know it's long past time for me to have a car of my own! I've been borrowing trucks and cars and sundry vehicles and driving them ever since I was twelve! I'm still borrowing cars! Hell, Esmerelda is beginning to think she belongs to me!"

I was extra mean to her because I knew that with a car of my own, I could have left that bad place earlier. I would've had a choice. Not having a choice earlier scared the hell out of me, but I wasn't about to tell her that!

Mama's face whitened, her jaw hardened. She shook her head no and wouldn't look at me. It was hopeless. I threw up my hands in despair and stormed on through the store, out the back door and headed for the fire pit. I couldn't figure Mama out. She knew I needed her permission to buy a car, even though I could pay for it myself.

Hell, I needed a car. Just one of the reasons was that I took back after my mountain relatives. Most of them had probably been driving since birth. My instincts told me I would I have no problem multitasking while whipping around mountain curves with a Camel cigarette dangling from my lips, hoisting a Black Label and drinking it down without pause, and basting whatever kind of pork was cooking on the grill welded to the driver's side of "Ol' Daisy." And speed. I liked it. I longed to crash an old battered truck through a curved, upward stretch of virgin mountain undergrowth while chasing bad people off of my land for hunting gensing on it and shooting at my pet squirrel Rusty.

I was sitting on a log, staring at the ashes in the fire pit, when I felt an arm go around my shoulder. It was Normaine. Eddy was with her.

"What's wrong?"

I sighed a gusty sigh.

"I'm so damn relieved to be home!"

"What happened?"

"I rode home with Leeza on the bus to her house. It was bad there, and I couldn't get away because I don't have a car, and I called Cowboy Johnson to come and get me and it took him forever!"

I thought about it a minute and said apologetically, "It seemed like it took him forever, but it really didn't. It was just a few minutes, but I was ready to run from that bad place."

Eddy and Normaine looked at each other.

"Yeah, we know about places like that. You're not planning on going back there, are you?"

"No way!"

They looked at each other again.

"Okay, here's what we're gonna' do kid."

Normaine looked to make sure no one else was around.

Eddy whispered, "Yeah."

"Your mother has a belligerent ghost," Normaine explained.

"What?"

"She's afraid you will find some reason to go back to your father."

"Never!"

"But she don't know that. And I don't think you can convince her of it."

"I'll go talk to her right now!"

"Go ahead, Dumbass! It won't do you any good. That will be twice today you've been a dumbass! That's the thing she's afraid of most in this world. Nothing you can say or do will change it until she realizes you're not a child any more, and most of all, that you will never have to put up with what she put up with. She's afraid he'll get a hold of you even after you grow up. Remember, you're the same age right now she was when he got a hold of her. Those dark people have power! You get a car; you might head right back there. And then her life wouldn't be worth living."

I stood up. "I'm going to talk to her right now!"

Normaine grabbed me.

"Listen to me, Dumbass! She won't hear you! She can't. She has to do it this way! There is no other way for her to do it. No options. This is non-negotiable stuff for her. She has to do it or die, that's how serious it is!"

"What?"

"Look, your mom has suffered enough. So have you. Let's just agree that she won't change about this, no matter what. Let's accept that as fact and go on around it. Like water going around a rock in the river. You still need a car. So, we make sure you have a car all the time, but not one that belongs to you. Right, Eddy?"

I groaned.

"You're tired of me using Esmerelda so much, aren't you?"

"Yep. We are. Just tell us how much money you got saved for a car, and we'll bring one home with us next time we come in off the road."

I stood there, letting it sink in. Then I cried. Normaine hugged me while Eddy patted my back. Poor Mama! She loved me so much! While I was crying, Cowboy Johnson stepped out the back door with two Cokes in his hand. As soon as he heard my wailing, he turned and scooted back in the door. I heard him say. "Jesus spare me! Teenagers! Can't tell from one minute to the next with them!"

I stopped crying and burst out laughing.

*

I took my money to Eddy and Normaine. Three hundred and fifty-seven dollars and thirty-seven cents. Eddy and Normaine held a secret conversation with William the Dude and Cowboy Johnson, after which they came to me and said that Cowboy Johnson would agree to say the car was his, that William the Dude needed me to run store errands in it for them.

My first car would be a store car. That way, I could use the "store car" all the time, without Mama fearing it was my ticket out of heaven back into hell. Halleluiah! I began having visions of swaggering out the front door and down the porch steps jangling my new keys on their new key chain bearing a rhinestone and mother of pearl emblem on it with "Geena's Wheels" engraved on it, while I strolled toward maybe a discreet little Thunderbird convertible in powder blue, or maybe a red and white 52' Cadillac, or a turquoise and white Chevy hardtop, or any of the other beautiful, classy cars I loved. Mine, mine, mine! Soon I would have my first car! What would I name her? I didn't know yet, though I was leaning toward something like 'Eleanor Posinvelt.'"

In a couple of days, Normaine and Eddy went back on the road again. "We won't be gone long this time," they said innocently, winking broadly at me.

I stopped harassing Mama about a car. I knew it was a torment for her to even think about me having one. I was taking psychology in school. Even if I wasn't, I now understood that odd wasn't a problem for us mountain folk. When Mama and I were together, we built up a natural anxiety trying to understand each other and find something in common to talk about.

Mama wasn't one for grocery line talk, she didn't like making small talk. It was genetic. I didn't either. Our mountain ancestry still hadn't made it past the short sentence. No dangling participles or extra adjectives there. This condition made our talks even more anxiety producing. People have to have a meeting ground, so I talked to Mama a little bit about being psychic and asked what she was feeling inside, and about astrology. That's the way the universe made her, and I accepted it.

All of us misfits were a little left of center and prone to bouts of depression. Children and dogs loved us whether we loved them back or not. We were what we were. It was interesting and fun for me most of the time, though I knew it was sometimes agony for Mama. Being of a scientific bent, I was not as susceptible to Awe as Mama was. It was hard for her to know the difference between Awe and superstition. That was genetic also. So many old stories circulating back in those dank, isolated mountains without any new input. Just the exaggeration of the old, and some fabulous biscuits.

The making of that particular Holy Grail was genetic with us too. That's where I became off the charts superstitious. My ancestor's rituals about biscuit making was set in stone, like the tablets Grandpa Moses or whoever it was, carried down the mountain to the supper table. The time of day biscuits were made was early morning, or just before supper. No fresh lunch biscuits. Those were leftovers from breakfast or supper.

Each biscuit was to be a large square at least three inches across. Each biscuit was to be tall and fluffy and brown and crisp on both the top and the bottom, and powder puff light inside when broken open by hand to apply a pat of real butter dead center. Biscuits were to be halved neatly, three corners loosened carefully before the fourth corner was used to pull it apart. Then it was to be placed just so on a plate, never in a bowl before milk gravy was ladled over it using a plain, every day tablespoon. No "gravy boats" or pouring it like some people do.

An old fashioned, hard used plain plate was advisable. The fragrance of delicious homemade biscuits brought out the satisfying, early morning courage of my pioneering forefathers in me. My generations of sweat and toil and DNA and genetics back in those mountains showed up every time I ate one of Mama's homemade biscuits.

Each time I ate biscuits and gravy, I had a hankering to go out and hitch up Ol' Bess, the mule, and plow and reap or sow, depending on which season it was. I wanted to hang hands of tobacco in a barn and run the grinder when it came sugaring cane time. I wanted to climb hills and cool off in creeks and silently dance the hoe down after drinking white lightning from a quart jar.

A yearning to drive fast and eat biscuits was the genetic foundation of my mountain heritage. More of my heritage was available, activities involving shotguns and bee keeping and root gathering, but I stopped at stringing green beans to make "shucky" beans and using wood clothespins to hang sheets on a clothesline. I would leave the guns and cussing to my male ancestry. But the car. I had to have the car.

I wondered what kind of car they would bring me. I had experienced the biggest disappointment of my life with Ray, and I was leery of yet another one, so I tried to keep my excitement down. I couldn't. And, I couldn't tell Mama what I was so excited about. She looked at me kind of puzzled, so I knew it would be advisable for me to channel my excitement into something possibly profitable. But what?

I gave it some thought. The Mafia sisters baked fruitcakes. I didn't mind fruitcakes because they were made in stages, not in a big, one-time stress filled production like a regular cake. I decided to bake cupcakes. Cupcakes were small, neat and tidy. Easy to make. Made in sections, just pour a bit of batter into each round little hole in the pan, and bake. Easy to frost, one at a time. I set to work.

"Why are you baking so many cupcakes? Planning on selling them?" Cowboy Johnson asked.

"Maybe. I'm baking them until Normaine and Eddy get home."

He got my drift, fast. He nodded and walked away.

"Ovens!" I heard him mutter. "Why the hell did God make 'em?"

I grinned at his back and kept on stirring the huge blue bowl of yellow cake batter.

The next day, Normaine and Eddy called the store for their usual check in. Cowboy Johnson leaped for the phone, shoving aside the cupcakes surrounding the phone. After a long, low voiced conversation in which he sounded a bit desperate, he hung up.

I baked more cupcakes and thought about life. We try to understand our bodies, our lives and our destinies because we think we own them. Well, we don't own anything, including them. All of those things slip through our hands with the passage of time and return to another way of being. Our wisdom is locked into our bones and flows through our blood every second of our life here on Earth. Mine was yearning for a new kind of independence. The kind a fine vehicle gives to its driver.

I kept baking cupcakes and thinking about life at Cowboy Johnson's Desert Oasis. My home. We were all fine as long as we were here. We were bright, shiny little empaths, inviting people to temporarily share our special stomping ground. But going out into the world on purpose took a different kind of grit. It took courage for a Sensitive to step out into this loud, bright, harsh world without retreating into muteness or migraine headaches.

Dreams are a large part of the vocabulary the inner part of the self uses to talk to the awake part of ourselves. I dreamed of Fords and Chevrolets and Edsels and Cadillacs and other cars. And Ray. And trucks. And Ray. I daydreamed about us riding in a Buick or a 1956 Powell Pickup truck with the windows down and the wind blowing through my hair. I baked more and more cupcakes and waited. Ray ate bunches of the cupcakes while listening to me whine about how long Normaine and Eddy were taking. Snow would fly and the desert store would crumble to the ground before they delivered my first car to me.

Then one day, without knowing why, surprising me and everybody else, I felt like crying. I didn't know why. The urge to cry and grieve something was so urgent it just burst out of me.

The crying started after I ate some cabbage. Why would I cry over eating cabbage? Sure, cabbage always stunk like a body removed from a shallow grave after three weeks' worth of decomposition when it was cooked, but was it that bad? Should cabbage be banned from my diet forever since it made me cry?

I cried for days. I cried over a wrinkled cactus and the empty rocking chairs on the front porch moving in the wind. I cried when the dust whirled up and threw itself like a cloak over the hood of William the Dude's gorgeous yellow truck. I cried over the fact that Mama would die someday, and I cried over the fact that I would miss her.

I couldn't bake cupcakes or wait on customers. I was useless. I wandered around feeling empty until the next tidal wave of tears swept me under. There was no end to it. No comfort. No one saying, "There, there, it's all better now."

One morning I was sitting on the front porch, waiting to cry again when Cowboy Johnson came out on the porch with a cupcake and a cup of coffee in his hands.

"Good morning."

He settled into a rocking chair near me, ate the cupcake, sipped his coffee. When he was through, he said, "You can let this thing pull you away from us to its side. If you do, it will get bigger and bigger, and you will lose us."

"What?"

"See that crow out there? It's making the rounds for early morning pickings. It's gleaning. It's finding what it can to eat and build, using what's here right now. It's not thinking about tomorrow, or days gone by in its life. Just today. I think you are crying because you are growing up. Hormones and all. Now you're waiting on the car, so it can carry you further away from us."

I burst into tears.

"Yes," I wailed.

Cowboy Johnson stared out at the gas pumps and the shade roof over them until I stopped crying. I was glad he stayed. I didn't want any hugs, and yet I did. I was caught between here and there.

"The car will carry you further away from us. That's the truth."

It was a flat statement. A true predictor of my future. I pictured myself driving down a skinny little road in the dark, all alone. I nodded in agreement, tears welling up again.

"And you will have to go. And we won't be able to choose where for you. We are not supposed to."

I nodded. New understanding flooded my being. My tears stopped in their tracks. I stared out at the gas pumps and the high roof shading them while inside myself, I moved on. My wild, itinerant heart longed for travel and adventure and new places ever since I could remember. And who I was before life changed me again, would be held in trust by these people, loved and guarded. I was free to go. To have my own set of wheels. He held me while I cried in that way for the last time.

"New times will come, and you'll cry again. Only different, and I'll be here."

I laughed and hugged him, and ran down the steps and ran back and forth with my arms stuck out like wings, shouting, "Whoooo, Whooo?"

Cowboy Johnson interrupted me.

"That cupcake was good. I think I'll have another. Want one for breakfast?" I nodded and raced back up the steps.

Chapter Eight

Yeah, don't let her old maid looks fool ya'.
my woman's allus' been an old maid,
a green fendered bad ass street rider
with plenty a' juice under her hood.
She passes ever' thing but a tent revival...
Look out then!

I groaned silently with disappointment. My new car was a four-door, dark green sedan. A 1953 Plymouth Cranbrook with a six-cylinder flathead engine. An old maid. Conservative and practical, with upright tan leather seats designed to straighten your back. An old biddy's car. That's what they brought me. I groaned again.

Eddy and Normaine shoved the car key into my hands. Then they hugged me and headed toward the store. I laughed and nodded and hugged them back, but my heart wasn't in it.

I told them I didn't care what kind of car they brought me, but I did. I imagined everything from a nice, conservative Mercury with hydra-matic drive, to a 1954 Hudson red convertible. I sighed and looked at the old lady car I was going to have to settle for. "At least it's a ride," I consoled myself.

Now it was up to me and the car to get acquainted. I sighed and circled it a dozen times before I opened the driver's door. The round dial speedometer went up to one hundred miles per hour. There was an AM-FM radio with plain silver knobs, the standard large steering wheel with the glove box in the center for easier driver access, and tan leather seats. I tapped the horn. It held the high, pleasant voice of a little old lady sipping tea. This car once took voice lessons from Miss Mississippi Delta.

I checked out the trunk. It was large and deep with a whitewall radial spare and a gas cap under the trunk lid. I walked back up front and ran my hand across the seat. It was smooth and gave easy. Just the right amount of elasticity in it. But it felt sticky. I frowned. And there were a couple of wadded up paper napkins on the floor of the passenger side.

I opened all the doors and the trunk. It was time to clean my granny car up. After I got her cleaned up, Cowboy Johnson came out, opened the hood and looked the engine over.

"What's her name?"

"Miss Gertie LaMars."

"Hmm...Miss Gertie LaMars is the same dark green as the El Camino."

"You mean Elsie, don't you? As in El Camino?"

He looked at me for a minute.

"Elsie... L.C."

"That will do just fine."

He walked off. No one could predict my reaction because of all the crying and stuff. Mama, who didn't know anything about the car, was just plain puzzled. Cowboy warned Eddy and Normaine. I could tell. So, they all left me alone with green as a Martian, my old biddy car, Miss Gertie LaMars.

William the Dude drove up and parked. He got out, grinned at me, winked, and ambled up the steps and into the store. He was inside telling Mama our made up story about Miss Gertie LaMars being a delivery car, no doubt. In a short time, they all poured out the door. Normaine, Eddy, Mama, Cowboy Johnson, and Ray, with William the Dude in the lead, and squeezed themselves into Miss Gertie LaMars.

I got behind the wheel and took us all for a first spin. I looked around at the laughing, bright faces in Miss Gertie LaMars. They trusted me and loved me completely. Even on the highway!

With my hands on the wheel, it seemed to me that love is the greatest liberator of them all. And these people brought me to this knowing through their love. Here I was, and them, riding along in the symbol of my latest liberation, Miss Gertie LaMars, who was a little solemn on the curves, but fast on the straightaway. Roots and wings. That's what they gave me. I began to sing.

"Home, home on the range, where the deer and the buffalo roam..."

I sang at the top of my lungs, and my family joined in.

"Don't anybody give up your day jobs!" I shouted at them when the song ended.

*

I picked Leeza up every morning at her ramshackle old house and we rode to school together, listening to the latest songs on Miss Gertie LaMar's radio. I dropped Leeza off at her house on my way home from school.

Leeza's family was large, dirty and proud. They all scowled threateningly at me every time I pulled up, except for Timmon, Leeza's youngest brother. I didn't care. I didn't like them either. I already knew too much about low down families, so I didn't ask her any questions. I just kept right on picking her up for school. I could tell she wondered about me sometimes, but she didn't ask. She knew better. I would tell her things as the time came right for each one, if it ever did with anybody.

We both kept our silence about the sad, bad things in our lives and focused on getting on with it. The only problem was, the bad things were still happening in her life.

Ray graduated. Summer vacation began. He was going to start college at Colorado State University in the fall. I spent all the time I could with him, so I didn't see Leeza much. Ray and I rode up and down the empty desert highways like vagabonds looking for a place to light. Like fireflies flitting about until their lights burned out. We were afraid to stand still or sit still or be alone, for we knew we would fall into each other's arms and do the unknown thing we thought about so much.

We ran through that summer, taking chaperones as hostages with us. We kidnapped the other misfits and held them hostage through long, dusty aimless road trips. Normaine and Eddy rode with us. Cowboy Johnson and Mama rode with us. No time to stop and hear crickets, no crawdads to watch, no shade trees, fence rows, tall grass, or shady bars reeking of booze to sit in and while away the time. Just the desert and empty space. Boring. But safe.

We drove the two Mafia sisters to church. We ran errands, toted supplies, and ran out to the ranch to visit Emma more often than she would have liked. But she had patience with us. So did William the Dude.

The summer wore on. Then it was time for the Fourth of July campfire. I invited Leeza and Timmon and a bunch of my friends to it. We picked Leeza and Timmon up and took them back to the campfire with us.

The two Mafia sisters invited several potential boyfriends. The four of them ate fruitcake and got happy from it and laughed a lot. It wasn't long before the two couples were holding hands and giving each other meaningful glances and sidelong looks.

I watched all that carrying on and got thoroughly pissed off. They could, but Ray and I couldn't, huh? Did this special kind of hormonal hell take place forever? At all ages?

I shuddered and strode away from the fire. I strode out to the highway and ran down it. When I couldn't run any further, I stopped, turned around, and moseyed back to the campfire. Ray, William the Dude, Cowboy Johnson, and the rest of the men were lifting fireworks out of cardboard boxes. Cowboy Johnson handed a box of sparklers to Mama.

I sat down and grinned at Ray. He was watching me and sorting firecrackers. I could never stay down for long. It just wasn't in me. I was like a bobber on a fishing pole that gets pulled down, but always floats to the top again.

The night wore on. Leeza and Timmon were supposed to be home by midnight. Mama and Cowboy Johnson were sitting side by side, stealing dreamy looks at each other. No one could endure like those two human Rock of Gibraltar's! They didn't laugh and talk like me and Ray did. God knows how they communicated. Psychically, I guess, although Cowboy Johnson didn't appear to me to be the sensitive, nervous, psychic type. He was more of a one syllable kind of guy. Yup. Nope. Maybe. Later. Who? What?

Normaine was watching Eddy light firecrackers, her black eyes sparkling. Then there was William the Dude and his lesser half. I didn't like her. I believed she would always be dangerous to him. I never could never eat much fruitcake anyway. I preferred Pepperidge Farm Double Chocolate Distress Cake.

William the Dude was helping set up the larger fireworks, while Algestine watched him like a hawk. I felt sad for him. He was too old now to ever get free. I looked around at my family. I was their child, at least for the past few years. They were my parents, mentors, and friends. They were Secret Keepers, Surprise Makers, and Cookie Bakers. They were Seers, All Knowing Cussers and Driving Instructors. They were Homework Helpers, Hair Brushers, Seers, and Teachers of Life.

I wanted to stay their child, but something in me was pushing me past them tonight. I stood up and stretched. My straight brown hair fell past my waist, and I still had my freckles and funny nose. My body was straight and tall and not much matured. I guess I was a late bloomer that way. But it made it easy for me to run. I ran in school and won races and medals. I never knew what I was running from and didn't want to know.

What Cowboy Johnson and William the Dude didn't know about old cars would fill a thimble. I knew how to change oil and flat tires, the many uses of a rachet, and how a carburetor worked. Ray, of course, already knew these high and exalted things.

"I think I teethed on a rachet," he joked.

I could see each particular strain that us odd ones, we Misfits lived under. Even though we did not often seek trouble, sometimes it found us. What I was and always would be, the misfits held in their hands. I knew that beauty and fear stood sharp in my face as stood up, thinking about the driving force leading me to consider deception. I was not good at deception. But I would do it anyway. I was going to sleep with Ray after we dropped Leeza and Timmon off.

Standing up, I stretched tall and lanky with my hair falling around me like tender brown rain until Mama came out of nowhere and grabbed my arm. She jerked me to her and held me and hissed in my ear.

"No! You won't sleep with him yet, and this is why! You must wait for the sanctity of marriage because of your father! It has to be clean and known! Please, wait a little longer! You can handle this. It's just hormones!"

Then Mama let go of me. I whirled away from her and Normaine's strong arms went around me. A waterfall of hair darker than my own shielded my face. Normaine pulled me tight to her.

"Don't let any man ruin your life for you, kiddo. Ruin it yourself, if you want to, but don't let somebody else have the fun of doing it to you Dumbass!"

I snickered and raised my tear stained face to look at Normaine, the lovely Indian goddess healer whose favorite healing word wasn't "Om," but "Dumbass!"

"Why can't we do like you and Eddy do? Pretend we aren't doing it when we are?"

I was furious at the unfairness of it.

"Why, you two act like rabbits! And everybody looks the other way. They pretend for you, why not for me?"

"Because, Dumbass, we are grownups and we were both married before. That means we already done it with somebody for better or worse."

"Okay."

I gave up, went back to the fire and sat down on a log. Cowboy Johnson, William the Dude, and Ray were standing together off in the distance. All of them were gesturing and shaking their heads. I'd watched them do this before. They were expounding their theories about something to Ray, like when they explained the resistance of wind flow across a car to us.

Ray was staring at the ground, his handsome, dark face flushed. There was a stubborn tilt to his jaw. I figured he was getting the "don't do it!" lecture, too. Well, great minds think alike. I read that somewhere. Evidently, he wanted the same thing I did. There was nothing more they could have done to convince us that we loved each other and doing the wild thing was the right thing to do. Positive or negative, they piled up testimony to our intense love for each other through their nay saying—almost like witnessing for us in a church.

We were constantly scolded and told what to do and how to behave by this lunch that humped and carried on like a pen of rabbits any time they felt the urge. No more.

The Mafia sisters disappeared into their rooms with extra fruitcake and their "friends." Indignant, our feelings hurt, we danced with the others, laughed, ate, and set off more fireworks. Then it was time to take Leeza and Timmon home. William the Dude stopped us and said, "If you're not back in forty minutes, we'll come looking for you."

He winked at us.

"Us old folks need you young one's back here to chaperone us, so we don't set anything on fire."

I had nothing to say to any of them. Neither did Ray. We just wanted to get Leeza and Timmon home in a hurry and figure out where to go to do it. Ray drove, and I stared up at the stars. My biggest fear was the disapproval of my family, not of sleeping with Ray. Those sillies! Didn't they know that the universe didn't revolve around whether Ray and I slept together? My Misfit family's spiritual form of hokey pokey was wearing me out.

I thought about my father. My father dreamed. I remembered him speaking of accomplishing impossible things. His father and grandfather both dreamed dreams that never came true too. Maybe it was genetic. Spiritually genetic. My father was a lost soul—one who turned inward to evil for solace, like a spoiled brat throwing a tantrum.

Sure, Good was sometimes hard to follow, but even though evil could disguise itself as easy, in the long run, you lost yourself to it instead of gaining yourself. To me, that was the most important difference between the two.

Sadness swept over me. I could never speak the "R" word, even to myself. Normaine and Mama were forced to have sex on a daily basis in their earlier lives. The big "R" happened to them over and over again. Day after day and year after year, they survived under the Shadow of daily "R". That's why they were deathly afraid for me, even though they finally got away, even though they knew I wanted a man who was good and kind, like the ones they had now.

Well, my own soul would just have to lead the way. I would not let it be held hostage to family fears or approval any longer. Maybe it wouldn't happen tonight because of their watchfulness, but it was inevitable. I relaxed and scooted over to Ray. Cowboy Johnson once told me the most important thing to watch for in people was who they became when they didn't get their way. Did they turn into a bargainer, a negotiator, or a manipulator? I watched very carefully for that ever since.

Cowboy Johnson held a good father's love for me. He said one could know the deepest truth of existence, but they still were to live their daily life because they were in human form, involving the usual frustrations and joys.

I giggled as I pictured God playing golf while nonchalantly munching on a ham sandwich, since He was the greatest Ham of all time, while ignoring all of the desperate suggestions rising up from the struggling people on the Earth below.

*

We didn't sleep together. Leeza and Timmon came to live with us instead. Then her mother and three sisters got moved into the motel by the Mafia sisters after one of their brothers tried to burn their house down late one night with them in their beds.

It didn't take me long to realize Leeza was a walking black cloud of self-pitying doom living in the flesh. Unlike the rest of the spawn of Satan, meaning her mother and sisters, she didn't have a spark of Hell in her. Which, at least could have made her interesting or maybe even likeable. Thankfully, she tricked us all, ran off with an old guy, then moved into the revival tent church with her mother and sisters. I was so happy to see them—and her—gone, that I felt guilty for maybe half of a second. She didn't come back to school and bother me there either. Life was good without Leeza.

Chapter Nine

Gimme' dat' ring and gimme' that thing!
I'm gonna' make an honest sumpin' outta' you yet!
What? You don't say?
ain't no preacher on the lost highway?
well, let's ride on down just a little bit further and
see...

My senior year smoothed out with Leeza gone.
Every time Ray was home from school, I tried to get
him to sleep with me. He wouldn't. He kept saying I
was too young. It was too soon. Wait. Wait. Wait. I
knew my horniness—I knew that word now, and the
full extent of its meaning was frustrating him.
Sometimes he took off without any explanation. I was
afraid to ask where he went. Normaine said he was
just visiting Madame Palm and her four sisters.

And so we waited until I came to believe that I
would die an old, gray-haired spinster on welfare,
living in a nursing home, bent and mumbling and
drooling and peeing on myself, which is what
Normaine said would have happened to her, if Eddy
hadn't come along and rescued her. Well, I wanted to
be rescued in the worst way!

I confided in Normaine, and she snorted.

"You don't need rescuing. I did. There's a big
difference!"

She laughed.

"Your hormones are roaring! You just want some
poontang, not love! Some sweet meat, not respect!

You want some sweatin', ruttin', fast breathin', load carryin', hot-time man stuff instead of romance and kindness! You can get that kind of stuff anywhere! Most are men willin' to do it any place, any time. But not your man! He's gittin' hisself eddicated' enough to deserve you. He's saving his self for you, and Madame Palm! Why, I don't know! And you's shore makin' it hard on him! Why, I know women who got fifteen men on the line to get that stuff from! One for every day of two weeks, and one extra just in case one of em' gives out!"

I ran away like always when Normaine started talking like that. But I heard her words. I held power over Ray. I didn't know what kind it was yet, but she was implying I better straighten up and use it wisely.

I took every class I could find having anything to do with bugs and insects and lizards. I studied biology, botany, and all the associated sciences. I learned that people who study insects were called entomologists, and people who study lizards and other reptiles, were called herpetologists. I wanted to be both, so I decided to study biology and become a wildlife biologist. There wasn't much available on the subject, so I sent away for college brochures, hoping at least one college would be out there in my chosen field. Bunches of brochures came in, and I spent a lot of time looking them over. I needed to take classes in zoology and environmental studies and biochemistry. Maybe I would become a biological scientist.

I finally found what I was looking for in South Carolina. But I didn't want to go to South Carolina. I wanted to go to school in Colorado with Ray. It was a dilemma. Then, just before Christmas break came, Ray made a short weekend trip home to announce he was going skiing in Aspen with friends instead of coming home for Christmas vacation.

"So, I will see you all after the New Year."

I thought, "Here we go again!'

Us misfits were all assembled in the back of the store when he made his reckless stupid, announcement. We were decorating the fake Christmas tree that served people in this treeless, desert part of the world as a make do for the real thing. People here put up fake Christmas trees, decorated them and took them down sometime after Christmas. Many people left their trees up all year because they missed having real trees around. If there was a real tree around here, and someone cut it down to use as a Christmas tree, they would be lynched, strung up and left to dry into human jerky in the desert by a mob of local folks. Coming home to Cowboy Johnson's store each Christmas was an imperative Law all of us misfits followed without question.

Ray tried to keep his voice matter of fact. But it didn't work. I heard the quaver in it. The tree was up with boxes of decorations sitting around it, when he told us.

He swayed back and forth, handsome and tall and lean, black hair crisp and shiny, dark eyes troubled. No flashing, white toothed smiles. No blushing making his skin turn into the most beautiful tawny shade of velvet I ever saw and forever yearned to touch. Ray was always bandbox neat, and he wore red this morning. It was his favorite color. We all knew by now that Ray tended to think things out alone and come up with isolated opinions. He enjoyed making announcements, like the professor he was to become. He also wanted to stick by them, like the professor he would someday become. We already knew he was stubborn as a mule about following the conclusions he drew from his self-centered thinking.

Normaine said, "Dumbass!"

I hissed. Eddy clucked and twirled his mustache while Algestine, Alena, and Aleda crossed themselves. William the Dude just waited. Timmon and Cowboy Johnson and Mama looked at each other. We all knew what each other was thinking. This wasn't the first time we were forced to take the time and patience to get Ray to include other people's thoughts, meaning ours, on what he was thinking about doing before he did it. Since Ray thought in black and white, it was always difficult.

Ray said defensively, "I'm thinking about becoming a Buddhist. They don't celebrate Christmas."

"The hell they don't!" William the Dude said.

"I lean toward Buddhism in spiritual practices myself." He raised a quick hand to stop Algestine's protest. "Regardless of what other religions are available. It's the only one I know of that that allows a person to include the practices of other religions in whatever way they need to. A very admirable thing."

He gave Algestine a long, cool look. She dropped her eyes, pulling her mouth down into a grimace. I wondered if he'd wheedled the fruitcake recipe out of her yet. I bet not. She was tougher than a boiled owl.

"Good luck buddy!" I thought to myself with sympathy. I guess I wasn't the only one to fall in love with someone obtuse enough to peel the bark off of a pine tree. Not that there were any pine trees around here.

Ray said, "Well, I believe in reincarnation too! It's the only thing that makes any sense! I mean, when I look at the layers of Earth in my studies, I know that the dust of ancients is in it."

William the Dude nodded.

"Me too. I believe in reincarnation too. Always will."

"Then why are you pretending to be a Catholic?" Ray asked him bluntly.

We all held our breath. William the Dude turned his light blue eyes and charming smile on Algestine, who was sitting there like she was a stone. Or a pillar of salt. Which I would have preferred. I would never like her. That day would never come.

"Because my lovely wife needs that from me. Simple as that. She has her religion, and I have mine. Shows up in two different ways, but we deal with it. She plays the bowls for me when I meditate, and I go to mass with her. Respect, Ray, that's what it's all about."

William the Dude grinned at Algestine. It was a grin suggesting that she smile back at him. She didn't. The two Mafia sisters looked everywhere but at them.

Cowboy Johnson said, "I'm glad you brought this up, Ray. The Christmas season is the right time of the year to think about spiritual joys and problems

and to try to solve them with..." he emphasized...
"...your family."

"Your sorry ass needs to be put in a hot sweat lodge!" Normaine interrupted his words. The two Mafia sisters sucked in their breath and primly crossed themselves again.

"You need to go to mass and confession!" Eddy said. "You need to go to the round church so the devil can't corner you; and take plenty of pasta with you!"

"No, take beer!"

"No, repent of your sins or go to purgatory!"

"Maybe a vision quest and a sweat lodge?"

"And a Spam sandwich...?"

Normaine turned and looked at Mama and me. A look of remembrance and wonder stole over her face.

"Oh, yeah."

She looked around while the two of us watched her and the rest shouted more suggestions to Ray.

"Quiet up, Dumbasses!" she shouted. Everyone shut up.

"This store was a church long before it was a gas station. Nobody knows for how long. We came here scared and half dead from other people working us over our whole lives and ate Spam sandwiches in this place. Cowboy Johnson fried 'em up crisp and just right and let us set on the porches with "out of order" signs on us while we healed. It's time to straighten up, Ray!"

"I didn't think you knew about the "out of order" signs," Cowboy Johnson interrupted.

I couldn't resist saying something, too.

"Yeah. You two almost rotted before you got better!"

Everybody laughed, including Ray.

"I remember those days," he said.

I read somewhere that we are all more alike than what we look like, but sometimes I wondered if it was less with Ray. Suddenly, we were all in sync again.

Mama said, "This place is a church disguised as a gas station and grocery store. There is something about the energy here in this exact spot on Earth that heals Misfits like us and brings us together to heal each other. We were all drawn here to this healing chakra center and it has healed many of our problems for us. We are a wise bunch of..."

She searched for words to describe us.

"I'm not touching that line with a ten foot pole," Cowboy Johnson stated dryly. "I'll just keep the fried Spam coming and stay out of it."

Everyone laughed. Then a long silence fell. After a minute, Eddy stood up and handed Ray an ornament. Ray took it and looked for a place to hang it on the tree. The crisis was past. Ray would go or stay. It was up to him. But we would all decorate the tree together. My heart both flew up and sank down into the depths.

Every person is different. And Ray was changing again. To love someone meant accepting their changes and not interfering too much. But my heart kept distancing itself in self-defense from the hurts he inflicted on me with his thoughtless, obtuse thinking. Each of the changes he thought about never included me. That kept me constantly scared and on my guard with him. The price I paid every day for loving Ray was high. It caused me to lose the location of my fun and chew my fingernails, a bad habit I took up again recently. Mama hugged me like she knew what I was thinking. She handed me an ornament and I put it on the tree.

To take the edge off my anger and hurt with Ray, who was once again acting like nothing happened, I deliberately thought about Keith Kincaid, my clever and funny lab partner in my latest biology class. Keith was ambitious. He planned on taking medical training and learning to fly airplanes so he could work with indigenous tribes in South America. He asked me out a few times, but I refused. If Ray decided not to come home for Christmas, then I might go out with Keith. I tried to picture Keith and I in a little two-seater plane flying toward South America, looking lovingly at each other. But my Sight didn't like Keith, so it liked him wearing huge goggles, and the plane engine kept missing, then went down in a blaze of fire while I parachuted out to safety. It didn't work.

Ray headed back to school after avoiding me for the whole weekend. He left without telling us whether he would be home for Christmas or not. By that time, I was through with my misery. It was time to take action.

I rebelled against my Sight and studied up on Keith Kincaid. He thought he was funny, and he talked all the time. But his voice grated on me and his personal habits left a lot to be desired. He snorted. And chewed gum with his mouth open. Was Keith to be a gum chewing, snorting, hijacking savior for me? A willing to liberate, detour of a savior with a bad haircut and roaming hands? A sacrificial god with straight "A's" and pimples?

Or would "Epic Ray", who seemed to think he was Moses reincarnated, never stop thinking ponderous thoughts about parting the Red Sea while he proudly and handsomely conquered the spirits of nations with his amazing wisdom, be my sacrificial savior?

Or would I end up being a spurned woman, one given up on being a wanted woman? Would I become icy, curt, and churlish, with withdrawn, sneering lips of spurned desperation whenever I encountered the world of men? Would I shave my head and leave my ears barren of decoration along with growing the whiskers of an old spinster someday?

At least I was smart and tough, and I was definitely not afraid of being a smart, tough girl. No eye fluttering, eye batting advertising for men, ball of Maybelline fluff here! If Ray Makepeace kept this up, my instincts told me I would inevitably reach a place where I wouldn't have much left in me to love him with. And that would never change because there would be nothing left to change it with.

Would Ray Makepeace become just a stranger passing through? A stranger who only stopped by to hang an ornament on our Christmas tree out of sentiment because he remembered the store from long ago?

Would I only get know him in my soul, this boy man who had dwelt in my heart for these many years?

It's odd about the sense of smell. How it takes a person back to another time instantly. Ray's boy smell had changed into a man smell. I missed the smell of the soap he used. I liked talking to him. I always wanted to know all about him.

I would be alone forever in a certain way if he left me. That's as far as I could think. Later I realized that the way he was had already left me, and everyone else alone. My thinking was simple back then. If Ray left us, he would be leaving the rest of the misfits too. We were part and parcel of each other. Did he remember us driving five hundred miles each way to deliver him at a special spelunker's camp for two weeks? Why, he was not just some guy who could wander off. He was our beloved Ray, we were not finished needing him yet.

I swept the store floor until Cowboy Johnson said the boards were getting so thin he could almost see through them. I ordered more clay than I could use in a thousand years, shaped it into lizards, and painted them frantically. I crisscrossed the desert and made camp fires every night, whether anyone wanted them or not. Mama said I was wearing a scowl the size of Texas. I scowled even more because she said it as though it was a dress or a pair of pants I could put on or take off.

I didn't believe this misery would ever end. Mama and Normaine dropped whatever they were doing and hugged me when I rushed by in endless flight. The Mafia sisters crossed themselves whenever I was near and urged fruitcake on me. Cowboy Johnson and William the Dude wisely stayed out of my way for I was mad at the whole male population for even existing.

Time dragged by. Eons and acres and miles of it. Then the asshole-jerk-moron finally came home on

Christmas Eve in the late afternoon. Talk about waiting until the last minute! He jumped out of his truck while my now almost soleless sneakers squeaked to a stop at the front door. I turned and fled through the store and out the back door and across the parking lot and in between the outhouses. I was on my way across the desert to Washman's Draw, and no one was going to stop me. I was a runner. I won medals for running.

I was waiting when he came running over the swell leading down into Washman's Draw. I stood waiting, feet apart, arms crossed. Not even winded. But he was.

"You've got to forgive me!" he shouted breathlessly. He skidded to a stop in front of me and pried my arms loose and grabbed my hands.

"Okay."

I won. If it snowed a blizzard right now, he would find me in it. If I was at the bottom of an ocean sporting long, wavy green hair and mysterious fins, he would find me. If there was a mountain between us, he would cross it or tunnel through it to find me. I could tell. I knew all of this with one swift knowing.

Power flowed through me. Wise woman power. Yellow with orange flame power like a 1961 Corvette convertible ready to rumble. Power like a mint green 1952 Hudson Hornet ready to lay rubber. Or a 1959 Desoto pale blue Fire Sweep Shopper station wagon filled with a furnace of lightning beneath its hood. Or a 1953 Packard Caribbean Matador in maroon waiting for the Holy Grail to be laid at its feet.

I was a hundred power women rolled into one. A Wonder Woman, Super Girl, Eleanor Roosevelt, Red

Sonja, She Hulk, Storm, and Vanessa the Weather Girl all rolled into one. All metaphors for the collected wisdoms my foremothers had invested in me genetically came together in this moment in time.

I looked up at the sky, expecting lightning bolts and thunder. I remembered the story of the Milky Way Mama told me one night when I was sitting outside with my chin in my hand, studying the stars.

"The Milky Way lives in the Great Cosmic Sea among the rest of the stars. When the Earth was being born, the Milky Way poured its light out of the sky to light the Earth's path. The Light was pulled down and absorbed into the four powerful Magnetic rivers bathing Earth through its first birth. Those waters still run today over mountains and through rivers and down to the seas. In some places, the Four Rivers are still and silent. In other places, the Four Rivers gabble around rocks and over cliffs. And there are some places where they roar so loud that Creation hears and listens to what they have to report.

Water retains all memories of creation and life. The light from the Milky Way residing in the Cosmic Seas match our emotional content and so those Light Beings chose to become our ancestors on Earth."

I stood there waiting. I knew what Ray would do next. At last I knew the answer to the question seeded into my being the first time Ray and I met. He was my soul man, my karmic companion through countless lifetimes. It was Karma. He knelt before me, brought out a tiny white box, opened it, and offered it to me.

"Close it," I ordered. He did.

"Will you marry me?"

"I will never marry you. But I will wear your ring, and someday be your lover."

"Why won't you marry me?"

"This is why. Because you will never love me first. There will always be a Dinah or a philosophy or something else waiting to be first."

I shrugged.

"It is in the nature of things for us to be who we are. And you need something very different out of life than I do. I need somebody to be first with, and you need somebody to be second to your needs. I can't do that. And I won't be hurt by those differences anymore. From you I have learned to keep something of myself in reserve for when I need it. To never give all of my heart to anyone again. I alone am responsible for my heart now."

I looked away and frowned with the weighty responsibility of my new decision. It felt powerful and correct. He'd forced me to grow up in a new way. I shouted at him.

"You can't come in my room ever again to look at bugs or for any reason!"

I watched him take a step back, his face filled with guilt.

"Okay."

I took the box from him, opened it and put the ring on.

Chapter Ten

I keeps a' knowin' ya's gonna' git' me in trouble...
ya' keeps a' comin' 'round here, I mean...
I cain't hep' ma'self nor complain
'bout any of it, 'cause I'm glad
I'm jist' a fool for your love, baby...

Ray Makepeace

I stood up and reached for her, but she turned and walked away. Something in my soul reared up and took hold of me the first time I met her. I stood perfectly still, watching her from the back porch of the store as she ran across the sand, a long, lean arrow, long, straight brown hair flying behind her. The closer she got, the more I noticed. Freckles and a straight nose snubbed a little bit at the tip. Eyebrows like sparrow wings racing above light blue eyes the color of aconite and the rosemary blooms growing in my mother Emma's herb garden by the kitchen. A full mouth, wide in smile, deep in dimpled corners. Skin the color of fresh, tan, smooth cream.

She ran up the steps, and lit like a soft, airy moth in the space in front of me. Sparkling eyes peered up at me in wonder.

"Who are you?" she asked me this in a young velvety voice. I stared down at her.

"How old are you?"

She bristled and then laughed.

"Not as old as you!"

I drew myself up to my full sixteen-year-old height.

"Well, I think I'm not much older than you are, but I certainly am taller."

She peered up at me.

"Not much. And not for forever. You'll see as we get older."

She paraded around me, sniffing and examining me with her eyes. This had never happened to me before.

"I'm Geena. Mama and I are staying here. Who are you?"

"I'm Ray Makepeace."

"William the Dude's son?"

"No. I'm William the Dude's grandson."

Geena laughed.

"Oh, yeah! We are surrounded by old fogies around here! Care to accompany me to see a rare desert bug I just found? The oldies hearts might give out if they saw it. Grab us a couple of orange Nehis will you? Unless you like Coke better. We gotta' hurry or the bug will be gone! Or they will find something for us to do."

She raced off the porch like a young colt heading for green pasture, and I raced into the store for two orange Nehis. That's how it all began. Or at least my version of it. Hers is different. And now here today, kneeling in the sand, a few years older but not any wiser, I was asking her to be mine forever, for I knew she already was.

I have never understood my Geena. She is forever a pagan, a star believer, a rush order fortune teller, a classic car fanatic who knows a carburetor inside and out, a clay lizard artist and painter like my mother Emma, a Spam eater, and a spaghetti lover. She is a bug and lizard chaser, a specimen hoarder, and world traveler. She is Royalty. The Duchess of Mysteries, a Lady of Light, the Marquess of Hastily Made Sandwiches, the Dowager of the strawberry ice cream freezer, and the Lady Bountiful of orange Nehi sodas.

When she rolls up to the house in her 1957 Dodge Royal Lancer, with its miles of chrome and blinding whitewalls, its fins quivering, my heart finally lifts into the better place it has been waiting to occupy. Geena is the only one who can take me there. She is an optimist. Always looking on the bright side of things. And I will love her until the day I die with all her faults.

And now there is Celia to love.

This is how we got Celia.

It was at Christmas time. Geena and I were sitting on the front porch of the store with Geena's Mama, rocking and drinking sodas, catching up. Cowboy Johnson was out back putting the finishing touches on something or another. We were keeping a lookout for Timmon, the designated driver for the silver toaster crew these days.

Grandfather, Algestine, and the two Mafia sisters were with Timmon. Their assigned rooms in the motel were ready for them. We drove Geena's Dodge from Carolina, and arrived at the store in New Mexico early in the morning. After we unloaded our stuff into motel room number four, next to the garden chapel, we wandered up to the store.

Time flies by so fast. We were home for Christmas once again. I tend to forget how open and welcoming the desert is, and how cold it gets on long winter nights. Geena and her mama's words ebbed and flowed around me.

"There is no snow."

"The roads are clear, but it is getting colder."

"We are going to have a campfire tonight."

"That's nice."

"How's school?"

Geena's Mama always asks, though she never has any notion of what either of us does in school.

"Good."

Geena nodded. Geena's Mama looked down at her empty hands. I knew what she was thinking. She craved blood grandchildren. Someone of her genetics to pass the legacy of Sight on to, I suppose. But we didn't want any. Our plans did not include children. Geena was adamant in her philosophy about that. The legacy of the Shadow she endured during her childhood changed her life path into one that gave to all children, never to her own blood, for part of that blood was her father's. That would be too personal, too hard to stand. Besides, we would have to marry, and Geena would never marry me.

I stopped feeling hurt over her rejection of marriage a long time ago, for she was totally committed to me. I was damn lucky. That kind of faithfulness was hard to live up to though, but I was good at compartmentalizing my life so she didn't see my moodiness or some other things that would have broken her heart. I took whatever she was willing to give, and gladly.

Cowboy Johnson and Geena's Mama weren't married either. I guess that bad man of Mama's up north and that bad dead one of Normaine's down here, made our family start a new tradition, because Normaine and Eddy weren't married either. Just grandfather.

My years of training were almost done. I would have my Ph.D. soon. Geena would have hers, too. We planned to take coordinating jobs and travel the world together. Before long, school wouldn't hold us back anymore.

We planned our intertwined lives neatly and easily. We were happy. I sighed in contentment and leaned back in the rocker. It fell over backward. I felt a sharp pain in my lower back.

"Oh no!" I groaned. I was so tall and lanky that many pieces of furniture did not fit me. This was not the first time I suffered a crash.

"Oh lord, there he goes again!" Geena said.

"I'm taking him back to our room and working his back over, Mama! You stay here and watch for them. We'll be back as quick as we can."

Geena helped me up and we wobbled through the store and out the back door. We wobbled across the parking lot to our motel room. She opened the door of room number four. I wobbled in, fell across the bed and groaned loud enough to wake the dead. Geena closed the door and started toward me. The pain was ebbing away, but I didn't let on. Geena carefully straddled me and began massaging my back. I tried to stay silent, but I finally moaned with joy. Geena heard the difference, and immediately stopped what she was doing.

Geena was a sucker for touch. I reached as far as I could reach, for a man lying on his stomach with a woman straddling him, and touched every place I could reach on her. She let me. I grew braver.

"Lock the door," I moaned. She did, and that's how we ended up having a baby after all. Spontaneous coupling got us in trouble. Changed our lives forever. Geena called Celia her the Motel Room Number Four baby.

No more big shot Ph.D.s traveling the world to help other children. Now there was child of our own to care for. Except for her sparkling black eyes which were like mine, she was a little girl so much like Geena that I could deny her nothing. Geena didn't want any more children, and I was fine with that. One was enough.

Geena and I were married one month before Celia was born. It took her that long to agree. But I needed the legality of being Celia's father. I needed my legal rights. Geena finally gave in. "Cutting it a little close aren't you?" the preacher asked us.

Now we were home again for Christmas, sitting on the front porch rocking in the same old chairs, watching for the California contingent's arrival.

Eddy and Normaine were in the store with Cowboy Johnson. Geena and her Mama, who was nestling Celia in her arms, and I, sat rocking on the front porch. The familiar conversation flowed around me.

"Looks like it might snow."

"Think so?"

"Maybe."

"We got a camp fire planned for tonight."

"Good."

"How's work?"

"Good."

"That's nice."

We were waiting for the right time to talk to Mama about watching Celia this summer while Geena and I went to South America on a dig. I looked around while I rocked. Nothing changed. Time seemed to stand still at this little store and gas station out in the desert.

Celia was four now. She stayed snuggled in her grandmother's arms. She loved the same way Geena did. Freely trusting, running with joy to explore another's offerings of love, accepting skimpy or large portions. Not like me. I was reserved and put a few orderly, sensible conditions on my love. I needed order. Geena came up with that conclusion, and the two of them, Geena and Celia, discussed it, and I was found to be acceptable. They may as well, because I am not changing who I am for anybody.

The two of them agreed life was a journey fraught with good and bad and possibilities. Like bobbers on fishing poles, they bobbed back up to the surface each time a negative life event pulled them down.

No such luck for me. I was one of the many suffering the realities of life, not the illusions. My path was much more painful than theirs. I required common sense and order and rules. I suffered guilt and shame over my secrets, though they were harmless enough. Everyone said I grew increasingly handsomer. I changed my shirt three times a day. If life was any different than this, I did not know it.

I never discussed any of this with my store family. They would fault me somehow. When the world got too small for me, I ran to find a philosophy to make my life bigger again. I always found one, through diligent searching. That was when I took solace with a short term friend to get relief.

Mother was on her way here from the ranch to wait with me for William the Dude, her father, my grandfather. Celia was the only grandchild for both Geena's Mama and my mother. Four generations of us together.

None of all the possible blood aunts and uncles and cousins any of us might have, knew where this miscreant bunch of misfits lived. I never felt like a misfit, like the others did. Still, I would help them keep their secrets from their kin. Where they lived and what they did was their own business.

I knew a few things. Cowboy Johnson and William the Dude met in California when they were young. Cowboy Johnson was quite a bit younger than William the Dude. They both came from serious money because of the natural way they acted. Nobody without money acts that refined and has those kinds of manner without having developed the background for it. I never asked questions. I just listened and learned. I was more of an intellectual than the other members of our misfit gang.

William the Dude's profound dignity and depth kept him out front, leading the way carefully through life's minefields. Timmon was like him. Cowboy Johnson worked behind the scenes in wise, quiet, vigilant support of the rest of us, while Eddy kept us connected to the charm in the outside world.

Algestine was like the Rock of Gibraltar, or a pillar of salt, while her two Mafia sisters, Aleda and Alena, were disapproving, scoldy, safe harbors that never changed, no matter what.

Geena was an Empath. Normaine bore the courage of a red hearted bull. Geena's Mama was a psychic, a foreteller of events and mysteries. She traveled where her heart led her. And Celia, our darling little Celia, was a psychic and a healer and God knows what else. Not much got past her already. We would find out more as time went along.

Chapter Eleven

Dares' dem' dat' thaink' they did a bestest' thaing'
raisin' me and my gizzard ta' run on empty,
but dis' daincin' fool ain't running on empty no moe',
nope, neva', not nohow.
Gonna' run and daince ta' my own tunes now.

I left that to the women to handle. I was glad of the diversion, for there were secrets there was no need for them to find out. It wouldn't help any situation for them to know about Stella or any of the others. Stella is part of the reason I get nervous when we come back here.

I wasn't smart enough back then to know not to pick someone too close to home. Dinah moved away. Stella and I got together two weeks later. I got relief and then got smart and dropped her fast. I started making trips elsewhere to see others to get relief. It was much easier when I was in college in Colorado.

I can say on my behalf that my time with Stella and the others kept me able to tell Geena no when she pushed me for sex. And she pushed me a lot. I stayed angry and frustrated at Geena for always pushing me. What was I to do? What was between me and them was just simple rutting. Like many other guys do. Much of it was ugly, all of it was low, but maybe some of them had reasons. Like me.

But all that's in the past now, and everybody has something in their past they have to live with, and parts they won't tell anyone. That's the way of the world.

Let's just say Stella made it possible for me to accept and never complain about Geena's locking up her old room. She still keeps it locked up from me as though she knows the secret path I walk. I atone for my guilt over being stupid for ever mentioning Dinah-too young to know better- every time I come back here by never mentioning that room.

Since all that was a long time ago, surely Geena will see reason and show her old room to Celia; at least someday. How ridiculous of her to not have done it yet! And yes, it would open the door for me to go in there again. A doorway leading back into the special place I used to share with Geena. Surely it is still there, waiting for me. Being the patient type, I will wait while Mama and Cowboy Johnson keep it locked up for her.

When Christmas is over, we'll go back to Carolina and resume our lives. But for now, we're on a mission. Geena and I have the chance to go to South America with a group on a dig next summer. But we can't take Celia with us. Well, we could, but it would be too dangerous. Too much malaria and snakes and other things down there.

I suggested to Geena that Celia stay with Mama and Cowboy Johnson for the summer. At first, she was adamant. No! Then, during one of our weekly calls to the store, Geena's Mama asked if Celia could visit and stay for a while before she started school next fall.

"Well, Mama, maybe you can keep her next summer."

Geena drawled her words out haltingly, examining their newness and the commitment they implied. I stayed out of it. A smart man would. Now it would get talked about before we went home, and hopefully, settled. We needed to make plans months ahead of time, and the University agreed to wait on our decision until we returned from Christmas vacation.

I glanced over at Celia. She was content to stay in her grandmother's arms. I knew from past Christmases that she would be happy to stay there until the first of forever. You see, Geena and I were never physically very affectionate with anyone else, including Celia. I don't know why. I suppose it has something to do with us both being professors; maybe living in our heads all the time. Being reserved.

Celia's grandmothers have no problem carrying her around like she is a day-old infant. And for as long as she wanted. I watched Celia's little fingers exploring their faces and hair and every other part of them she could reach, and them tucking her in with them at night.

Emma takes a room at the motel so Celia can spend the night with her and not be far away from Geena. William the Dude loves the ranch and spends as much time as he can out there. The rest of us caravan back and forth from the ranch to the store loaded with fruitcakes, food, and other stuff.

Mother is an even more prominent artist now, with shows in faraway places. Emma Makepeace. She travels more than she ever did. She is gone from the ranch frequently. But she always comes home for

Christmas to be with her generations. Us. Me. Her only child. And grandchild.

Geena was getting a special surprise this Christmas. She was nuts about certain models of old cars, and I found one that was perfect for her. I take several of the daily newspapers from this area. I found the right car for sale in the want ads a couple months ago. It was a sage green 1941 Oldsmobile convertible with a dark tan top and a magnificent art deco chrome front grill. The owner was driving it up from Texas to the store for me. It would be a perfect companion for Geena's 1957 Dodge Royal Lancer. I would her to drive something newer someday. I hope a different car will be a start. Her surprise is due to arrive two days from now—on Christmas Eve, in the afternoon.

I watched Geena get up and place a blanket around Celia's shoulders and sit back down.

"Looks like it might snow."

"Maybe we'll have a white Christmas."

Celia jumped up, ran down the steps and twirled around, looking up at the sky.

"Mama! Snowflakes are falling!"

She spread out her arms as if to embrace the sky. Then she stuck out her tongue to catch a snowflake. Geena ran down the steps and twirled in a circle and stuck out her tongue too.

"Come on!" Celia shouted, motioning to me.

I smiled down at her.

"It's okay for you to do that. Children do those things."

Geena stopped and frowned at me. Then Celia stopped and frowned at me. Two frowning faces. I stayed in my seat. It would be unseemly of me to join them. Wasn't it enough that I approved of their momentary silliness? I sighed. Boxed into the same old corner by Geena once again. This was happening a lot lately, and I didn't like it.

Just as Geena started to speak, her Mama stood up and danced lightly down the steps. She took each of them by a hand and danced them around while she smiled at me in encouragement.

"We'll go inside and warm up and have hot chocolate in a minute, okay?"

Oh, hell! I was being forced to do things, as usual. I ran down the steps and joined them.

$\acute{C}$hapter Twelve

Bless my soul! what's da' matta' wid' me?
I'm a' mean mota' scooter gittin' ready ta' flee'
Gittin' skinnier and madda' too
Cause' I'm half dead from this long ass ride
Gonna' stop someplace and step inside
Til' I'm fat and steady agin'
an' damns' good and ready ta' comes back out!

Geena Makepeace

"You'll catch a lot more flies with honey than you will with vinegar," Mama said when Ray and Celia went inside to be with Cowboy Johnson, Eddy, and Normaine and the others waiting for the special assortment of fruity Christmas cheer the Mafia sisters always provided upon arrival.

We were sitting in the rocking chairs again. Mama studied me and waited.

"Are you feeling okay?"

"I'm just tired, that's all."

A long silence fell between us. The snow started coming down harder. I knew it wouldn't last long. After all, this was the desert. So many things said without words while we felt out the differences between us. Some were the same as last year, others were different. I sighed again as I felt Mama's familiar psychic presence, her healer's examining ways. Gentle but probing. Then she pulled it away.

"Old Doc Peabody is coming by later to pick up a couple of things. We'll see what he says."

I didn't protest. I didn't care anymore. All I wanted to do lately was sleep. I yawned and shivered.

"I'll walk you back to the motel room."

We ambled around the side of the store with Mama holding me like she hadn't done in a long time because I wouldn't let her. Not since before we left that little Podunk town up north and set out on the road that eventually led us here. Being an untouchable back then kept parts of me safe from harm. I guess I still had the habit.

She unlocked the door to the motel room, went in and turned the heat up. Then she closed the door and helped me undress and get into my flannel pajamas. She tucked me into bed like I was a child. Then she went out, closing the door behind her. For an instant, I saw the falling snow through the door before she closed it. Then I fell into a deep sleep filled with dreams of being lost in snow and blizzards.

I woke up, then moved from a warm, cozy fetal position onto my back. I looked around the motel room. The walls were painted a soft peach. The bed frame, nightstands, dresser and chairs, and small table were handmade white pine. The upholstery, curtains, and bed covers were made of material with small, colorful birds sitting on branches or flying in a cheerful, lemony background. The Berber carpet was short napped, a desert tan, broken up here and there with Normaine's colorful rag rugs. Lemon, peach, and white towels were rolled up in a wicker basket by the back door. Old magazines, coloring books, and crayons lay on a shelf with book classics lined up like soldiers near them. On the table stood a small, deep purple glass dish filled with Christmas ribbon candy.

I glanced at Mama's Big Ben alarm clock on the table. I slept hard for three hours. I looked at the dim light coming through the curtains. It wasn't dark yet. I lay there in the warm silence, thinking about nothing. I could do that when I came back here. Nowhere else. When I was here, I became happy again, reverting back to the girl I once was, back when we discovered the store and Cowboy Johnson and the rest of my lovely family of misfits.

I ran my hand along my hip bone. I was thinner. A little more each year. Ray said it was just my baby fat leaving. We stayed busy with students and more studies and Celia. Early starts and late nights each day. Weekends filled with frantic makeup time, Ray reading the newspapers, me playing with Celia, trying to make up for not seeing her more during the busy weeks that fled into years. Now she was four.

The door opened quietly, interrupting my dark thoughts. I sat up in bed. It was Mama with Doc Peabody behind her. Mama was carrying a pot of tea and a mug.

"Red raspberry tea. Still your favorite?" Mama asked. I nodded. She set the mug on the nightstand and poured the tea. Fragrant steam rose from it.

"Yours just as soon as Doc Peabody is done."

I nodded again. The doctor quietly and quickly prodded and poked around, drew some blood and left. I picked up the mug and sipped.

"So good!" I murmured to Mama.

She smiled.

"Let's get you dressed."

After I was dressed, Mama poured me another mug of tea.

"Not so happy these days, dear?"

I buried my nose in my cup so I wouldn't have to answer. Her sympathetic energy filled the room, and I felt the last of my hardened defenses against her not protecting me when I was little begin to disintegrate. Why now? Why here? I asked myself. I felt hot, acid tears filled with the chemical emotions of a long ago time burning paths down my face, toxic tears hiding, waiting for years to escape their prison of buried grief. I never wanted to hurt Mama or anyone else. I should have been able to go on, never falling apart like the rest of the world. I groaned.

"You can't go on living like you are, or you will get dreadfully sick. Not just a little sick, like now," Mama stated firmly.

I burst into tears. She held me and I sobbed out waves of tears and sounds in between rubbing her arms and blowing my nose. I blubbered out old disjointed words from childhood and scrubbed my hands over the bed covers in anxiety. Finally, I wound down. Emptied out. There was more. But it would be different. This piece was lurking in the background since I was a little girl. Now I could think straight again. Suddenly, I wanted the days back when we first got to the store and discovered our lovely family of misfits. I wanted them back so much I grieved and shook with it.

Mama brought water and a fluffy white towel and dabbed me here and there. Then she helped me dress, like I was a three-year-old. And I let her. My heart was open again. Unexpected. Vulnerable. Suddenly, I was scared.

"You father is not here, remember?"

Mama spoke with certainty in her voice. She hesitated just a second before she spoke again. "He hasn't been interested in us for a long time. He divorced me and got remarried to a girl not much older than you. He stalked the school grounds and found her when she was in ninth grade and he was thirty-one. She is an only child with wealthy parents, and he has stolen her soul and perverted her to his ways. He could do this because she was so young. He hasn't been turned in to the authorities because you would have to deal with him again, and it isn't time for that. May never be. You still need that protection."

I stumbled over to a chair and sank down into it and stared up at Mama in wonder.

"How...?" she interrupted me.

"Cowboy Johnson hired a private detective. Dan Swain."

I barked out a laugh at his name.

Mama said, "Dan keeps an eye on him. Twice a year, his detective agency sends us an update on him."

Mama hesitated and looked at the window.

"Do you remember Bud from the gas station back there? He used to call me Map Girl."

I thought about telling her about Bud and the money I kept from her all of these years but decided not to. I nodded.

"Yes. I liked him."

"Well, Bud meets with Dan every few months and catches him up on what has been going on with everybody in that town. Nothing is ever put in writing." Mama shrugged.

"Bud and the detective have made friends and keep in touch with each other."

"How long have...?"

"As soon as we knew you were going to have a baby. We knew we could protect you, for you are older now. But a child? We needed to know what he was up to. I don't expect any problems from him, for he wants his wife's money, so he doesn't have to work. She supports him while he plays sick and illiterate."

Mama sighed, waiting for me to take it all in. Gratitude washed over me. She spoke with her back turned to me.

"I don't want to talk about this again unless it is necessary. Wherever you live on this God's green Earth, I will do the best I can to take care of you. It may not be enough sometimes, but that's just being human."

She began to fluff me up.

"Let's not talk about it anymore, okay? Now or later, unless it is absolutely necessary. The less we think about the old bad stuff, the better off we are."

Mama pulled me to my feet. We hugged each other. Then she helped me put on my coat and boots and wound a long scarf around my neck. I let her. I was grateful.

"It's still snowing, baby, but not heavy yet. Let's go to the store. They should be here soon."

As we started toward the door, we heard running footsteps and the door flew open. Normaine and Eddy rushed in. They skidded to a stop and assessed the situation with shrewd eyes. Then Eddy let out a shout of laughter and swooped me up in his arms. I was a head taller than him and I dangled everywhere, but he carried me out the door and headed for the store.

"We're like Popeye and Olive Oil!"

We laughed and I dangled even more.

"I'm like spaghetti."

"You keep that up, and I'll have to drop you!" Eddy warned. I grabbed him and looked around.

The ground was covered in a thin coat of white.

"It's so pretty! I want to touch it."

"Sure."

Eddy dropped me, and Normaine, who was following us, threw snow on me. I threw it back. Suddenly I felt weak and fell back in the snow, breathless.

"You okay?" I heard Cowboy Johnson ask. He knelt down and picked me up in his arms. I remembered being twelve and jumping out of the Merc' and leaping into his arms. I hid my face against his chest just the way I did back then. He carried me up the back steps and into the store and grinned down at me.

"Want to sit on the "Hideous Green Sofa"?"

I nodded.

When did you find out we named it that?"

He put me down and turned away.

"I'll never tell. Hot chocolate coming up. Who wants some, so I'll know how much to make?" he said, leaving me to ponder the mystery. Cowboy Johnson is my father. And now Mama was my mother at last. Part of the mystery was solved. But what about the hideous green sofa?

Chapter Thirteen

Hot, swanky sweatin' love, and smooth runnin'cars...
leave out the prowlin' tom cats and the sin bars
whatchu' got left? Nothin'! yeah!
Damn it! Jist' women, children, debt
and macaroni and cheese...

Ray Makepeace

Geena was taking a nap. Again. I was bored to death. Cowboy Johnson suggested I call mother and offer to go get her, so she wouldn't have to drive in the snow. I called before I drove out to the ranch in Cowboy Johnson's new truck, a dark green 1950 Chevrolet Morrison Farm truck, outfitted with snow tires and the works. He sure liked those green cars and trucks. Mother insisted we walk the ranch in the thin, falling snow and share old memories.

"This will be your ranch someday, Ray. Probably not too far off in the future."

I protested silently inside while I nodded and smiled at Mother. I didn't want my roots to call me back here. Not for a long time, if ever. There was too much for me to do, too many places to see. Besides, the psychology books said that kind of ordeal was a middle age crisis, and I was far from being middle aged.

Later, I put mother's luggage behind the truck seat, and we wandered the back roads to the store. The seats were black leather, very comfortable, the heater nice and warm. We arrived at the store just as Timmon pulled in towing the silver airstream trailer behind him. Everybody jumped out and started hugging and shouting and laughing. Then Timmon pulled the Airstream out back by the motel and parked it, and everyone unloaded their luggage into their motel rooms.

I carried mother's luggage to her room and placed it inside the door. She was too busy holding Celia to pay any attention to me. I studied them for a minute. Celia was my ticket to never losing the ranch, to never upsetting mother so much she would disown me. Celia was good security, but I still wasn't going to confess or tell anyone anything about certain parts of my personal life. It was my business.

I knew William the Dude would get his turn with mother, after Celia. Four generations of Makepeace's together once again for Christmas. William, Emma, me, and Celia. I whispered the names to myself in satisfaction.

Everyone gathered and moved as one toward the back steps of the store. Geena was inside, sitting on the Hideous green sofa, sipping a cup of hot chocolate. Delight and laughter filled the back room of the store like it did every year.

I sat down to nurse a cup of hot chocolate and study the faces around me. William the Dude looked older, but hale. Eddy and Normaine were gaining polish from living in the Big Apple. They wore black. Normaine wore huge silver dangling earrings that swooped around each time she moved her head. I watched her hug Geena. Her huge earrings got tangled in Geena's long hair.

"Damn it, Normaine! Those things could be used as lethal weapons!" Geena complained. They both snickered while they extricated the earring from Geena's hair.

I looked everybody over and felt content. Then my eyes went back to William the Dude again. Then to Geena. They both looked off somehow. Both pale. I felt consternation growing. Things needed to stay okay, so I could go on with my plans. Just then they hugged each other and laughed, asking each other questions and catching up. I sighed with relief and went back to my hot chocolate. Celia came over and I gave her the requested sip of chocolate before she scampered away. They all ranged around like a herd of cattle, moving from one person to the next, playing catch up, hugging and laughing and talking. Our family was back together again.

The skimpy snow stopped falling at dusk. Celia went with mother to her motel room to spend the night. The Mafia sisters retired to the Airstream. William the Dude and Algestine went to their motel room, followed by Geena to our room. But I wasn't ready to go to sleep yet. It was only nine o'clock, and I was used to burning the midnight oil. Timmon sat down and we drank some beer and talked about baseball. Then Cowboy Johnson closed the kitchen.

"Got to get up early to fix the breakfast. You boys ready to turn in?"

We understood the signal. It was bedtime. We shook our heads yes, stood up and wandered out the back door. The night was cold and clear with a three-quarter moon shining. The ground reflected the moon's light off the couple inches of snow that fell earlier.

Timmon headed for his room. I slipped quietly up the steps and into mine and Geena's room. She was sleeping soundly. I took off my clothes down to my tee shirt and skivvies, pulled on flannel pajamas and slid in beside of her. She was warm. I scooted up tight against her and ran my hand down her hip out of habit. Her hip bone felt more prominent. I used to not feel it at all. Oh well, maybe she was just trying to keep herself pretty and thin for me like those models in magazines. Didn't she know yet that she would always have my love? Women. I fell asleep.

The day before Christmas Eve day sped by. It was filled with trimming the tree, breakfast, lunch, dinner, in between trips to wrap and hide gifts, making a camp fire and roasting marshmallows. The car would arrive tomorrow.

The next morning I woke up. Skimpy snow was falling. The window curtain was pulled back. Geena was gone. I shut the motel room door behind me and jogged the distance between the motel and the back porch of the store.

I looked at the bacon, sausages, scrambled eggs and toast on the table. I smelled hot coffee and maple syrup. Cowboy Johnson and Timmon were cooking. They hadn't asked me to help. Well, good! I was off the hook!

I rubbed my hands together, grabbed a plate and sat down. I was hungry.

The morning passed swiftly. I looked out the front every little bit to see if the car was here yet.

The car arrived near one o'clock. The driver's ride back home pulled in behind him. I checked my watch in satisfaction, and guided Geena away from the crowd and up to the front of the store.

"Who's that out there?" I asked innocently.

"I don't know....but that is one fine car!"

The driver and a young man I took to be his son, were walking up the front porch steps. I met them at the door and ushered them inside.

"You Ray?" the man asked.

I nodded. He handed me the car keys and turned to leave.

"Wait! What are you doing?" Geena asked. I handed the car keys to her with a flourish.

"Merry Christmas, my dear!" I said to her. By this time, the gang was gathered around us. They all started talking at once. Geena started for the door, but Cowboy Johnson stopped her and frowned at me.

"You need your coat on, Geena. And gloves. And boots."

He looked at Geena's Mama.

"You. Take care of it."

He stepped to the back of the gang. I was puzzled. Normaine wound a scarf around Geena's neck, while Normaine slipped her coat on her. Celia brought her a pair of boots. Then the gang went out to look my Christmas gift to Geena over, while Cowboy Johnson offered the two car drivers hot coffee and fruitcake.

"That is one fine machine!"

"Great lines!"

"Great color combination!"

"Beautiful!"

Their chorus of voices urged Geena to start the engine while they piled in the car.

"I'll ride. Somebody else drive," Geena said, and climbed in the back seat with Normaine's help. Eddy drove. I rode in the front passenger seat. After a short ride, Geena asked to go back to the store. Eddy expertly executed a U turn.

"Sorry. I'm still sleepy for some reason," she apologized. A chorus of voices offered consoling explanations, but I wasn't buying it.

"You don't like the car," I stated flatly.

"I do!" Geena protested weakly.

"No, you don't. I'll sell it and you can buy whatever else you want with the money."

I huffed at her. Eddy gave me a murderous glance.

"Shut the hell up!"

"Yeah, Dumbass!" Normaine added. I looked back at her in surprise-and growing anger. Celia climbed on her mother's lap and hid her face. Geena's face was pale with rage or something. God knows what I had done now. Yet again. Over and over, I was made wrong. I huffed. Wasn't it enough that she threatened my dignity in front of teachers and students? Wasn't it enough that I lived with that daily threat? All the times she was impetuous and too familiar with me, instead of minding her manners and treating me properly, paraded swiftly through my mind. No wonder I slipped the traces once in a while. At least it was always with a sensible student, one who knew her place.

This was the last time I gave her a gift in front of this gang! My bank account was fat and full. Next time I had the urge to better someone, it wouldn't be Geena! I glared at her. She closed her eyes and leaned against Normaine's shoulder. What a pity party she was throwing!

"We'll have you back to your room in just a few minutes."

Normaine spoke soothingly to her, like she was a child. I didn't understand what the hell was going on. I wished to hell I was back in Carolina where the kind of sanity normal people understood, reigned.

"Is this good enough for you?" Eddy parked the car.

"Sure. Whatever," I answered Eddy with disgust and resignation. I jumped out of the car, leaving the bunch of them that did seem to know what was going on, behind. I stomped up the steps, went inside, poured myself a cup of coffee, picked up a book and started reading. I would have gone to our motel room, but Geena was headed there.

I always kept a book handy in self-defense, for this was not the first time this family of mine left me in the lurch as far to what was going on. But I knew I would get over it quickly without any discussion. I would forgive them. Forgiveness without explanation was one of my strongest traits.

Maybe Geena was getting sick. I didn't want to catch anything, so after the Christmas dinner, I would drive out to the ranch and stay with Emma. At least she appreciated me. I opened my book and turned to one of the great philosophers for consolation.

Chapter Fourteen

A few times in my life, ah' gotta' tell ya'
I busted my soul all ta' hell halleluiah
cause' a' lovin ' in wrong places
allus' a' pickin' a handsome lova' who
likes slippin' dem' traces
each time I ties a red ribbon 'round my skinny ass
ankles
and smooths on new red lipstick and smiles
that's what I does. Yeah.

Geena Makepeace

Mama slid over by me.

"Eddy, please drive around back to Geena's motel room."

Mama sent Celia into the store with Normaine to make me a bowl of Campbell's chicken noodle soup, while she helped me into the motel room and into my pajamas.

"I'm fine! I'm just so tired," I protested. But Mama wasn't having any of it.

"You are going to bed and sleep after you eat some soup."

She fussed around until she found a classical music station on the radio. She turned it down low. I closed my eyes and listened, remembering the days of Cowboy Johnson's Victrola and the good father he was and the carefree girl I once was.

The soup came. I ate a half a cup of it and crawled into bed with a cold orange Nehi on the nightstand. Mama left the curtains open and I dreamily watched the snow falling and closed my eyes.

I dozed off and on until after midnight when I sensed a change in the energy. It was Christmas day. A holy day. There were so many people on the planet celebrating Christmas that the beautiful energy of this day became holy. Twenty-four hours of beauty of the soul, filling halls and homes and cathedrals and stopping wars and healing the sick and uplifting humanity with new hope to live on for another year.

Ray lay warm up against me. I slipped out of his embrace and out of bed. I pulled on my hot pink robe, went to the window to watch the thinly falling snow. The wind picked up some, rattling the window.

I ran my hand through my short, thick, straight hair. I would never get used to it being short. I cut it for Ray, who insisted I was more acceptable to my peers with a short, modern haircut.

I thought of Celia, secure in knowing she was sleeping nearby and warm, snuggled up to someone who loved her. There was a long list of people who loved her, beginning with Mama and Emma and Cowboy Johnson.

I wrinkled my nose in thought. Maybe I was just coming down with a cold or something. Oh, well. I couldn't think straight right now. Maybe later. I went back to bed and fell asleep until I heard Ray getting dressed.

"Getting up?"

"Not yet."

I heard his sigh of frustration and shut it out automatically, as usual. I yawned and turned over. No more questions came my way. Just the sound of the door shutting in a few minutes.

I was a soul in torment. Perishing from I knew not what. What was happening to me? Would I die from the spiritual malaise hidden under this illness? Out of mercy for Mama and Cowboy Johnson, who was my father, and quite a few others, I wanted no record of what I survived as a child to ever be spoken of.

Out of mercy for Celia and Ray, I stepped even farther into the bright sunshine, leaving the Shadow behind. I locked the door to my old room and never went in there again. I locked it up just before I moved to Carolina. The past in that childhood room held the old Mama and my biological father.

It was a teenage girl's room. She lived there for a few short years. Or so I thought. But by staying in the Light, blessing and complimenting the presence of all who came my way, I exhausted my soul. Worn myself out. I stayed in the light too long. Right now, I didn't give a damn. I was in survival mode. I just needed petting and eating and to sleep.

I was beginning to understand what Mama and Normaine must have gone through when they slept a part of their lives away on the front and back porch of the store.

Whatever it was, I never questioned that it was bigger than the both of them, like this situation was for me. It was taking me over, no matter how hard I fought it. I sighed. I never wanted anyone to have to help me handle the darkness of me. And I never wanted to handle the darkness of others.

But there was Celia now, and my former carefree life that was so easy when it was just me and Ray, was gone. I once closed myself off as only youth can do, and let it stay that way for a long time. Maybe hibernation was a natural way to heal some things.

The door opened and closed. I heard the short, choppy whisk of the wind. I sat up and watched Mama carefully place a bowl of hot chicken noodle soup on the table, then go to the window and look out. The snow was coming down harder.

"After you eat, let's get you dressed, and up to the store. The weather is getting worse. It looks like we might be in for a good snowfall!"

I sniffed. The soup smelled good. I sipped a spoonful. It was delicious. I put the spoon down.

"Mama, what's wrong with me?"

"I don't know yet, aside from overwork, and not taking any time for inner thinking, so you can keep your spiritual strength up. You do know it requires a maintenance program like everything else."

She waggled her finger at me and grinned.

"You're too busy honey. That's for sure."

"But I am thinking of the old bad stuff, and I can't seem to help it, Mama."

Mama jutted her chin out in a familiar way.

"People tend to think about negatives when they are under the weather, like you are right now. Just tell 'em to go to hell and back off. That should work...Unless you're ready to confess to a bank robbery or to being the one who burned the teacher's papers in the cafeteria wastebasket..."

She smiled at me.

"Sometimes having a little touch of something causes you to give pause to your life so you can change directions or regain your health. Or it just means you got a damn cold or bug and will get over it soon."

"Mama, you sure do like to cover all the bases... But what if I said I never wanted to bring out the bad stuff that happened to me as a kid into the light of day? What if I still don't?"

"Then you don't. It does hurt other people to know it. But when you do bring it out, it gets resolved somehow with their help and healed. I can tell you this. Ditching that crap, however you do it, leaves you having a future space to be happy in. Some people hold on to their crap until they die, hollering for someone to fix the wrong that was done to them. Don't do that!"

She leaned over me.

"So, go forward Geena, whatever it takes. We're here. We'll always be here. That's my advice. I'm thinking we can handle it."

She turned back to the window while I finished my soup and stared at her back. Crap was a new word for Mama. I never heard her use it before. It gave a different meaning to the negative stuff I was worried about. She waited until I finished the bowl of soup.

"One final thing, Geena. You father moved on. Celia and you are forever safe from him. Not from life, but from him. We both moved on and got our lives back in two very different ways. He moved on in a certain way that we couldn't tolerate, and that is his karma. And you and I are happy and clean and

Good. That is our karma. Whatever Force runs the show is taking care of us very nicely. You'll see it that way as soon as you start feeling better. Also, Celia needs different Christmas socks to wear because the ones she has are too abrasive for her understanding."

Now who else would have put it that way? Who else would have attached a common pair of socks to Celia's spiritual growth? I laughed. Mama grinned at me.

We both knew I needed to watch it with Mama, because on the rare occasions when I did let her mother me, she let all kinds of pent-up wisdoms pour out on me. She helped me dress, then we strolled through the wind and snow to the store.

The tree was bright and sparkling, the big open back room warm with cooking and laughter. A small table was set up by the Hideous Green Sofa. The long folding table was set up nearby. The tables were covered with festive tablecloths depicting evergreens, Santa, and Rudolph. The tree was heavy with the ornaments we collected over the years. Mama guided me over to the Hideous Green Sofa. I sat down. Cowboy Johnson placed a mug of hot chocolate in my hands.

"Here. This will warm you up."

I took a couple of sips and leaned back. I was safe here from the Shadows chasing me. After a while, I started to doze off. I felt someone take the mug from my hand. Then I felt a warm quilt being put over me. I stretched out on the Hideous Green Sofa, listening to the sweet sounds of love filling the room.

Rumbles and soft laughter. Celia asking a question. I felt surrounded by love. Gratitude filled me. I closed my eyes and wept silent tears. A part of me was desperately tanking up on the love energy here because of the emotional starvation I endured in my life back in Carolina. A life I refused to examine and set right. Refused to, out of hope and a forever love for a dark, beautiful, roving eyed man.

I felt a feather light touch on my forehead. I kept my eyes closed while Mama's familiar hand checked to see if I had a fever. I knew I didn't. Mama and Normaine consulted in soft whispers above me.

"No fever?"

"No."

"Is she going to have to do what we did?" Normaine whispered. "Become a moron?"

I snickered inside at Normaine's choice of words.

"I don't know," Mama answered.

After a pause, Normaine whispered, "Maybe she's discovered his soul is too cold to ever connect to the heat of true love."

"Maybe," Mama whispered.

"But he loves her and Celia as much as he can love anyone."

"What do you think caused his coldness?"

Normaine whispered, "Hardship?"

Mama whispered, "Nope. On the contrary. Nothing has happened to him in this lifetime. It is a condition from his past life, one he carried with him into this life. Everything has been too good. No big trauma's to work out. It's just the way his soul came in this lifetime. It's running his show. It looks to me like his soul is searching for a cause to be involved in this lifetime instead of working out personal development through having a family."

"The dumbass!" Normaine whispered back.

"No. It happens to every soul that comes here, eventually. The soul has to learn its lessons too and evolve. She chose him because she needed someone with a cold soul to get past her bad father."

Mama spoke sadly. I lay there in shock. So that was it!! It all fell together.

"What do we do?" Normaine whispered.

"We look out for her and Celia. And try to put some fun into this life we live."

Normaine giggled.

"He is handsome and means to be kind, even though he's such a dumbass!"

They moved away from the Hideous Green Sofa where I lay huddled under the quilt.

I slept off and on for the next few days while my energy repaired the psychic wounds delivered to me through the disappointment of Ray's skimpy, cold way of expressing love, and my new understanding of my childhood wounds. They were deeper than I ever thought. I once believed I could turn my back on them, throw them away. I would have to have help healing. I knew that now. I could no longer walk alone.

When I got back to Carolina, I'd call my friend Valerie. She was a therapist, but I would never go to her; she was too close to me. But I knew without a doubt she could refer me to someone good. A woman. That decision made, I turned over on my side.

Now I understood why I chose him. I needed to choose someone beautiful enough to draw me and bind to them, to keep me focused on beauty, or I never would have been able to marry, to get physical, to get past my childhood. Beauty caused me to make the leap. And, I required someone with a cool soul, so I could tolerate a sexual relationship with them.

Ray owned a cold soul, and it healed me in many ways. But it wouldn't get any better than it was. That was okay. Celia and I would have to settle for a pompous, aloof love that didn't understand a damn thing about us and didn't want to. He couldn't stand our warmth, our passions. One person can only offer so much to heal old wounds, to remove old evils. Ray had been very successful in doing that job.

My family of misfits were the companions we needed. They were hot and rowdy and vibrant, like we were.

My father and his family and Mama's family were no part of our lives, and I never wanted them to be.

Now I understood what was going on. I knew some of what to do. The words Mama and Normaine spoke, their prophesy—I suspect deliberate—brought me to the place I could begin the journey out of the old dark place a young girl once lived in.

I fell asleep and my Sight informed me that I specifically worked with the vertebrae, with the spines of people and creatures. Bones and stones. Lizards and gizzards. That was why I studied lizards and so forth. The voices of the guides, angels, and other unseens, instructed me until I fell into a stupor and slept. I could imagine them saying, "Well, it ain't much, but that's all she can handle."

Ćhapter Fifteen

Sometimes ya' thinks your life's gonna' be the same
foreva'
then ya' gets evicted from it, ha ha
then ya' has ta' git' yo' bony ass out an' make a new
one!
but ya' cain't feel too bad, ya' shudn't,
cause' ya' knows ya' still got them fine, skinny, bony
ass ankles to walk it with!

Christmas vacation passed in a blur. I slept
through most of it. The doctor returned and said all
that was wrong with me was that I was anemic and
needed to eat more meat, especially red meat.

"So, she needs half a beef, a side order of fries,
and a Coke?" Normaine joked.

Mama and Normaine told the guys what the
doctor said. Cowboy Johnson and the rest of them
set up grills on the back porch and grilled things all
day long. I sampled everything. It was all delicious. I
ate steak for breakfast, burgers for lunch, and ribs
for dinner. The meat helped. I was tall and big
framed. I was off of my feed for a long time without
realizing it. I was a skinny Minnie. At last I started to
feel steady inside.

Ray spent most of his vacation with Emma and
William the Dude out at the ranch. That was a relief.
Celia rode back and forth between the store and the
ranch where she was very wanted by both.

It was the day before we left for Carolina. The weather was bad. A long drive lay ahead of us. Snow was piled sky high across the states we went through to get back, with more predicted. It was the snowiest Christmas season on record for these parts.

Ray handed me the keys to the sage green 1941 Oldsmobile convertible with its dark tan top and magnificent art deco chrome front grill. I hadn't named her yet. She was parked out back of the motel. I just didn't have the energy to drive.

"You can follow me. I'll lead the way out of the snow. Celia can ride with me."

Normaine and Eddy, Cowboy Johnson and Mama, and all the rest gathered around us. A huge silence fell while I blinked up at Ray. Then all hell broke loose. Normaine snorted.

"Dumbass!"

She shouted the word at Ray.

Ray turned to her. "What?"

"I said you're a Dumbass, if you can't see you have a sick wife on your hands! Dumbass, Geena doesn't have the strength to drive around the corner, let alone clear across the country following you! They got blizzard conditions clear to Carolina and tons of snow!"

They all nodded. Rays handsome face grew red, then pale under his olive skin. I could tell he was deeply offended.

"What the hell are you talking about?"

"You bein' dumb as a rock!" Normaine yelled.

Cowboy Johnson and William the Dude looked at each other.

"That's enough for now, Normaine," Cowboy Johnson spoke calmly. Normaine stopped and turned her back to Ray and embraced Eddy.

Cowboy Johnson said mildly to Ray, "You probably didn't notice the situation because you were out at the ranch taking care of things. But this little lady is under the weather and still recovering. The doctor was here, and says she is anemic and needs plenty of rest."

A look of shocked pride crossed Ray's face. He turned to me in a calm, icy rage. I was dumbfounded by the whole thing and didn't say a word.

"Why didn't you tell me?"

I didn't have an answer. A long, silent moment dragged by. Then Ray wilted. He sighed and turned to the others as his handsome, dark face became carefully expressionless.

"So...what do you want me to do? I have to be back at University no matter what. So does she."

Cowboy Johnson answered him in a careful, slow drawl.

"Celia and Geena can stay here until better weather comes and Geena is well again, or you can drive the three of you home in one car. It's up to you and Geena to decide. But the new car is not going to be driven home by Geena, or anyone else here. I believe Geena has some say in this matter, too. "

There would be no more castle building in the air. No more thinking things were different than they were. I needed to follow this man. I spoke up before things got worse and I lost him.

"We will go home with Ray. Mama, can you keep "Miz Liz Elf Mercantile" until spring?"

Everybody laughed at the name I chose for my new car. It broke the ice, and the new plan fell quickly into place. I would return for "Miz Liz Elf Mercantile" in the spring. Ray was hasty to go along with the new plan, and I knew why. We looked at each other thoughtfully. Both of us were thinking of the summer trip the University was offering us—as a team.

I knew he was thinking about how to pawn Celia off on this misfit bunch for the summer while I was thinking about how both Celia and I could stay at the store for the summer. No more castles in the air. I was learning a new, dark song. Sometimes Darkness restores what Light cannot mend. And I would make the dark, invisible forces beautiful as I would manage to do with my childhood Shadows. I would dance reverently on the grave of the Old One and sneak a Milky Way candy bar to my bad self to delight in while I drew snowflakes under new Shadows with the precision of an Einstein. Well, maybe. We would see.

I would train Celia and myself in the nourishing art of Unpredictability. So would Mama. We would live and flourish under a Wild Sun and a Curious Moon. We would make messes and mistakes and fix them through the methods of the women's wisdom encoded in us down through our generations, for we couldn't repair anything following the hollow, staid intelligence Celia's father bore.

We would distribute Favor, and eventually fall out of love with the fears we clung to. We would play to our strengths and be astounded when we encountered new ones. We would tend to our weaknesses and be gentle with them, for every weakness has its own way of kicking ass, for each one held the virtue of causing a person to rethink and change their position in life. Sometimes it was give in or die. Strong stuff. Personally, I did not want to mess with, or understand, the universe or Karma. I just wanted to keep it simple. My philosophy was that we needed beauty as well as tapioca pudding to survive the meanness of life.

We needed love the way we needed it, but we might have to go without it for long stretches of time. We would just have to wait until we were back at Cowboy Johnson's store with our misfit bunch of angels, eating fried Spam sandwiches and Pepperidge Farm cakes and drinking Nehi Orange sodas to tank up on love—a certain kind of necessary to life love again.

We would and could accept Ray as a husband and father. We needed him, and we would love him and let him love us back in the ways he knew how to. It would have to be enough. It was just the way of the world, and the way different kinds of loves worked. That was all there was to it. I chosen his soul for good reasons. I was okay with it all now.

We rode home with him, back to Carolina. He was kind and thoughtful to us. Carolina was home to Ray, but not to me, ever again. Cowboy Johnson's Desert Oasis would always be my real home. The little white church disguised as a gas station and store had been converted into a permanent home for us Misfits. I knew that now.

Meanwhile, I lost my ambition for academia and most everything else. During the next few months back in Carolina, I slept most of the time. The things important to me before didn't have a hold on me anymore. Nothing much did. Just Celia. I walked slowly through each day in an absent-minded way.

I felt distant, like I was an actress playing different roles in my life. I wanted the sweetness of sleep and Mama's touch, and a million more little things that I once rushed past in my hurry to survive, to stay grown up from being forced to grow up too young. My early life forced me to become old before my time out of necessity, and now I needed to tarry along awhile, to find out what I missed out on.

I became swamped in nostalgia. The sweetness of a candy bar, the pleats of a long ago little girl's skirt, were what I thought about when I sat down to do my paperwork. The fragrance of Mama's soap drifted across me at odd times. I imagined the notes of Cowboy Johnson's voice playing across the smell of frying Spam when I made lunch for Celia. I pondered the dryness of William the Dude's short, humorous epistles about life and what they meant, and stared out the kitchen window at the yard. The changes slowed me down, and I wasn't on schedule anymore.

One day, my Sight led me into remembering the reason why I studied bugs and insects, so much so, that I teach it. I was in South America several years ago, working with a small tribe of indigenous hunters and gatherers living on the Amazon.

They did a soul retrieval ceremony and allowed me to participate. There were about twenty of us. The Shaman gave us tea, then we laid down and closed our eyes. He took us on a journey I never will forget. We were to follow him single file and stay behind him on the Path, and stay on that Path no matter what happened.

Then he told us the three survival rules of following our Paths. The first one was to not give gifts or take them if they were offered. The second was to not touch anything and to keep our hands to ourselves. The third was to run away from any kind of bugs or insects if we saw them, because they were indicators that we were off our Path and were no longer protected.

Laying on that red clay dirt back in that village, I finally knew my path. I learned about bugs and insects so I could use my Sight—with my job as one of my disguises—to lead others back onto their Paths. I could heal spinal disorders because of my studies.

My Sight was different than Mama's. Mine was not as gentle and spontaneous. Mine was a warrior woman's Sight. I was learning about deliberate forms of protection.

My father back in Ardenville courted evil. He flirted with it and minimized it. Everything he encountered was filtered through a set of lenses that automatically rationalized and sympathized and minimized the evils in this world, especially his.

But Mama and I didn't get caught by evil like him. We ran away. I knew now that many people never leave. They get trapped or like it. I was glad when he died. I felt vast relief. There was no mourning. Just gladness that he or his perverted, enabling sidekick of a wife couldn't whitewash his sorry ass for him so he could hurt even anymore. I had read about Stockholm syndrome. I carried my lack of grief to

Cowboy Johnson, and he said it was okay. He said there were people in his family he would never grieve over either. That it was natural and good for us to be the way we were about evil, bad people.

I needed to learn and become strong and help others. I needed to mature beyond where I was. I needed to stop steeping in my hurt like a too strong tea and mature beyond where Mama stopped. I knew she couldn't understand. It would always be too painful to talk to her about it. She wouldn't be able to stand it without it breaking something in her. I never wanted that to happen.

I am Mama's daughter and always will be. We're both psychic, but we stand in different places with our Shadows. I am and always will be grateful for the gray, for the gray gives a place to practice and learn about Mercy, which is, I believe, one of the finer components of a larger lived life, for it has been served to me in good measure in hours of great need.

I mulled over that time in my life. The change began when I was in South America. Little by little. Piece by piece. By the time I came back to Carolina, I had distanced myself from Ray. The blinders were off. I understood his kind of love. I knew he would stray, but he loved me and Celia and always would. I knew now that his personality and strong ego consumed him and led him where it would. Whether he wanted to follow it or not was another matter. It was none of my business now. He was a soul on his own.

No doubt he would continue to whine and nitpick and let his quick, impatience flash into temper wherever it would. But I no longer needed to placate it. I couldn't. I wondered if he was like his father because he certainly wasn't like Miss Emma.

I called Miss Emma. We chatted about Celia. Then she said without preamble, "You called for a reason. What is it?"

A long silence on the phone.

"I want to know about Ray's father."

"Why?"

"Because he looks like you, but he is nothing like you. Is he like his father?"

Another long silence ran down the phone line.

She answered reluctantly.

"Yes. He is very much like his father."

I waited for more.

"Barron Swift is his father. He is an actor. We were married for a few months. He left before Ray was born."

"Barron Swift. An actor."

She heard the question in my voice and answered it.

"Barron." She spelled his name out for me. He is a minor Shakespearean actor who probably still treads the boards of little theaters around the country. He may have returned to England. I was one of many, and imagine I still am."

"What does Ray know about him? He has never mentioned him."

"Unfortunately, he flew the coop as soon as he heard I was pregnant."

"Oh."

"Yes. I divorced him immediately after Ray was born. The law wouldn't let me until then. Father started the divorce for me the day Ray was born. The old leaving, the new hope beginning. I never saw him or mentioned him again, and Ray has never asked. I suppose because father has always there his father-grandfather. He didn't seem to miss having a father. I guess he doesn't think about him because we never spoke of it."

"Oh."

"Barron Swift was a beautiful man with a personality that thought it was a law unto itself. No doubt still does. Those types don't change." Emma said dryly. "He may try to get in touch someday. He doesn't know me as Emma Makepeace. He knew me as....someone else. The name I was born with. I changed my name after he left. So did father. If Barron ever recognizes me, who I am, my real name, he may show up in our lives again. I am becoming more well known, so it's entirely possible. I will face that possibility if or when it happens. Father and I aren't worried about it; never have been. We are thoroughly legally and emotionally protected."

"I'm sorry Emma."

"Thank you, Emma."

I didn't have to explain to her why I was asking. She knew. We chatted some more about Celia and hung up.

I paced through our huge, daunting formal house, rearranging things, trying to make it more amenable. I asked the staff to bring in cut flowers. I pulled a large white mixing bowl out of the kitchen and set it down hard in the middle of the huge blond, blank square of wood table in front of the twelve-foot sofa and filled it with flowers.

"More green! I want leaves and stems, too!" I cried out. "Here, let me show you!"

I grabbed a pair of cutting shears, threw open the double French doors to the patio at the back of the house and ran outside. I looked around. It was too big for me. I needed to go back inside. This work was internal. It needed to be done inside.

"Just cut them, please."

I retreated inside and resumed pacing. My thoughts came thick and hot. At last I let myself do whatever it was I needed to change in this place where I lived. I pulled and tugged furniture around until the huge room was rounded out. Not a formal square of stiffness any more. By that time, Ray was home. To his credit, he didn't say a word. He tried using exasperated sighs and body language on me, but I ignored him.

I spent the next week shopping, ordering throw pillows and shawls and wind chimes, small sculptures and bowls, placing them around the huge, silent, formal house.

When Ray turned to me in the night, I stayed cool and still and he left me alone. Nothing was said about the change in me. He knew he was guilty. He was afraid to question me.

During the next few months, I attended faculty parties with Ray. I held his arm and beamed while I stalked the parties searching for Goodness in another man. Ray had it, but it wasn't mine alone and never was. I needed someone just for me, like it should have been with Ray. I never found anyone.

I walked through the big cold mansion we lived in observing it. It was out of order now. There were lovely pastel shawls and throws spread across formal, stiff furniture that refused to soften. The wind chimes looked lost and small in the vast windows, and the little clay people hid their closed faces behind screens, potted greens, and vases.

I went off on tangents when I taught classes and stopped socializing with the faculty. Ray was astounded, then dismayed. He became angry and huffy with me. At first he scolded, then he tried encouragement, then he began telling me what I stood to lose with my erratic behavior. Ray's anger and incomprehension, tempered by his puzzled love, clouded our days. I had no answers to give him. No emotional exercise to cling to. Nothing.

Ray raced past me in the world of academia, and before summer, The University took me off the job offer in South America. Ray was to go alone.

I was secretly glad and very relieved. He left early in June amid the hustle and bustle of suitcases and looks of disapproval directed at me. He ignored Celia for the most part.

Ćhapter Sixteen

Whatcha' gonna' do when da' well runs dry?
well, honey bunch, dare's mo' dan' one kind a' well
in dis' ol' worl', ain't dar'e, ya' fool!
git' on wid' it, I says
put some mo' tread on ya' bare tares'!

A few days after he left, Celia and I packed up. We stowed our luggage in the capacious trunk of "Gracie," my 1959 turquoise and white Dodge Royal Lancer, my spectacular land yacht with fins, showy whitewalls and miles of chrome, and headed out for the store. Miss Gertie LaMars, my modest green 1953 Plymouth Grand Brook with her six-cylinder flathead engine, had gone the way of fond memories, long ago. I drove slowly across the country, for I still wasn't back to myself all the way. It was all of eighteen hundred miles to Cowboy Johnson's Desert Oasis. So far away. I remembered my runaway trip with Mama, the freedom we felt. I felt that freedom again. Celia was fine. She was used to two distant parents making sure she behaved correctly and used proper manners. I watched her through the rear-view mirror. She was quiet and careful and sat still, looking out the windows. A little girl who behaved like a tiny, proper professor. She'd learned well from her two proper parents. She was beautiful and solemn, with Ray's dark eyes and my straight, brown hair. She loved books and hid in them ever since she learned to read. Correction. One formerly proper parent, and one absent proper parent.

I didn't know if I could bear the truth of the awareness growing in me or what it would bring. I never wanted this unexpected growing, causing an unending grief and soft triumphs that became a part of the ancient dirt the hallowed Earth is made of. Sweet and dark, sometimes to the point of nonfunctioning in this world, where I formerly functioned on a high scale with much approval. I did not want to join this club, and I fervently hoped this ordeal would be over soon.

Would I lose all of my hormones and grow wrinkles? Would my voice change into that of a Harpy? For sure, I would not be able to travel too fast, like a speeding bullet, like I did from the time I married Ray. That was over. Instinctively, I knew something inside me had slowed down permanently. Not from illness, but from being tired of the life I was living. It had up and quit on me. No two-week notice, no "I'm moving to Pango Pango", nothing. There would be no revving up the engine into overdrive to climb that mountain again.

I recalled a famous, cute little story about transformation. Well, that story wasn't mine. Mine was full of crap and misery. Instead of feeling like a butterfly floating around, my days were now one solid mass of molasses in January. Instead of smoothing out like a road of fragrant butter, I trod with previously unknown insouciance, like the psychologists predicted, I stayed depressed, low, and slow.

What caused this crap change? I liked the way I was before. It was easy and comfortable to follow Rays lead. Was it apathy, or complacency from a part of me that understood what was going on, but was keeping the information all to itself, while the rest of me was trying to keep the farm together?

Does life make its own choices, and take us along with or without our input? Who the hell knew? I just knew I was involved in a forced evolution with no turning back. I had grown too damn tired of too many things. The eastern religions talked about opening slow to life–the lotus blossom that unfolds slowly so it didn't kill you.

I was physically tired, too. After a while on the road, I realized I needed help. Celia was with me, and I didn't know if I could take care of her because I didn't know what was happening to me. That realization scared the hell out of me. I stopped at a gas station and called the store from their pay phone.

"Hello?" Mama queried.

"Mama, did you know that Ceoldefia trees, pronounced like Philadelphia, God knows where they started out at, maybe Philadelphia, hence the name, I haven't finished my research yet, are rare and ornery among tree types, only nine left in the world, grow sideways at ten thousand feet on the south side of the French Alps, and mature at three feet high at which time they poop green resins down their sides, coating them and releasing a stench that carries as far away as South America, maybe, no one knows yet, which scent vaporizes, and, if they are lucky, only scorches the long, hairy tongue of the Freezer

Band Beetle which populates its bark after their fermenting is done?

I finished and sucked in one long breath.

Mama said, "Geena?"

She knew immediately something was wrong. Maybe my voice gave it away. You never know when you are dealing with a psychic.

"What's wrong?"

I sighed.

"I'm coming home. Me and Celia. I'm in Georgia. Just got started good. Thing is, I'm not sure I can make the drive."

I didn't list the reasons.

"Hold on," Mama said. I heard her place the phone on the counter. The familiar sound brought tears to my eyes.

"Where's Ray? Is he gone already?"

Cowboy Johnson's familiar voice calmed me down, like always. As long as he was in the world, I was less afraid. A rush of love for him poured over me. My eyes filled with tears.

"Yes, my dear father. I can't explain the plight of the Billy Bong Beetle and how its scent became attractive to the flea population in Pago Pago right now. Too tired. I'm on my way to the store. Home. With Celia."

"Where are you?"

"In Georgia at a gas station."

Tears spilled from my eyes.

"And I may need someone to help me drive the rest of the way."

A long silence.

"Sorry."

I spoke apologetically and started crying. Then I stopped and took a deep breath.

"Tell me what to do. I thought I was still strong, but I am not a shadow of my former bossy self and knowing the longest walking mantis in the world is on the endangered species list for emitting too many different kinds of spit isn't helping."

"Okay. Ask the gas station people where the nearest motel is. You have money, right?"

"Yes."

"I'll wait."

I put the phone down. Before long, I picked it up again.

"The Blue Bell Motel."

"What's the address?"

I read the address the gas jockey wrote on a scrap of paper for me.

"I'm in Georgia," I said again. "In Twining."

"Okay. Go check you and Celia into a motel room and don't go anywhere. Get some food and magazines, whatever, but stay right there. Sleep and eat and shower but stay right there. Somebody will be there as soon as we can manage it, okay?"

I sighed gratefully.

"Okay."

I wasn't sick, but I was afraid. The unknown loomed so large it overpowered my competence and common sense. I checked into the Blue Bell motel with Celia. The room was large, sunny, clean, and threadbare. Next door was a mom and pop restaurant. Celia asked me why we were stopping.

"Oh, those silly people that love us so much from the store want to ride with us the rest of the way."

She studied me with her dark, sparkling eyes and finally nodded. We walked half a block to a grocery store and stocked up on snacks, coloring books and crayons, Little Golden Books, and an umbrella Celia insisted she needed for privacy, walked back and settled in.

If she knew better, she didn't say so. We went through a long night and most of the next day and all the coloring books before the hot pink Cadillac with its top down and its mile-long acres of shiny chrome pulled up in front of our room and stopped. Esmerelda. Esmerelda was here. My trance broke. I leaped for the door.

I had been staring out the window in a daze, not seeing anything but the emptiness of the parking lot. But one can only meditate upon an asphalt parking lot just so long without falling into a catatonic stupor. I had almost achieved that state of asphalt Zen.

Normaine and Eddy were here! Normaine got out of Esmerelda and posed by her while Eddy got out. I jerked the door open. Two pairs of shrewd eyes studied me. I waited in front of the open motel room door for their verdict. I knew I would be found wanting. The moment ended when Celia rushed past me shouting their names and threw herself into Normaine's then Eddy's arms.

We packed up and left. Celia rode in Esmerelda with Eddy. Normaine drove my wheels. Fifteen hundred miles to go, then I would be home. After we were on the road, Normaine looked over at me.

"Dumbass!" she stated, and grinned. I grinned back at her , and promptly fell asleep. I slept most of the way home. We stayed at a motel in Arkansas and one in Texas. Standard motel rooms with double beds. Normaine tucked me in like I was a child, and I fell asleep listening to Celia's questions and giggles as Normaine and Eddy told her bedtime stories having to do with sappy whappy toads or paper kites talking as they rose into the sky.

Finally, I saw the Store in front of us. Normaine drove in and parked. Mama ran down the steps and grabbed me through the open window and started crying. Normaine jumped out and came around to Mama.

"Celia is waiting for her hug, Grandma!" Normaine shouted in Mama's ear and backed away with a huge grin. Mama released her death grip on me and rushed toward Celia.

"I drew you a picture, Grandma," Celia said shyly.

We went inside. Celia led the way into the safety of the Store with her child's prattle, her doll Daisy cradled tightly in the crook of her left arm.

Cowboy Johnson scooped her up in his arms and set her down on a barstool at the long counter. Then he placed the required tall, cold glass of chocolate milk in front of her, went to the Victrola and put on some Debussy for me. I never played music at home because it irritated Ray. He said he needed quiet to think.

I sighed with relief. Suddenly, all was right with the world. Me and my child were taken care of. Ray? I never even thought of him. He was fine, I knew. I was home; there was no thought past this place. I was going to stay here. Maybe forever. Maybe for a shorter time. I didn't know. Or why I needed to.

"I'm going outside," I announced. I needed to be alone. To think. They watched me anxiously. I knew they wouldn't let me stay out there long. It was a sort of test I was handing them. I knew it, but didn't know what it was about.

I went out and sat down on the front porch. William the Dude rolled to a stop just after I sat down. He strolled up the steps and over to me. He took my arm and pulled me up into his arms.

"I'm gonna' make this quick. Let your hair grow long again so you can hide in it like you used to. Celia's got your hair. Teach her that trick, she might need it some time. It is a portable, attached benefit. Use what you got, I say. Okay, I'm done. Let's get you back inside."

Chapter Seventeen

I'm a' knowin' fo' shore;
I allus' got mo' travelin' in me
fo' findin' mo' tales ta' tells my honey chile'
until she's a' knowin' too, that hell,
ever damn minute, knowin' ever damn life
is a' makin' a hell of a story.
You got one too, chile,
so shut up and set in the sun awhile
til' you's'll figur' out that ya' cain't leave hell out.

We went inside. Mama took me in her arms, then led me into Cowboy Johnson's living quarters. She guided me down onto the familiar Hideous Green Sofa and sat down beside me. Neither of us said anything. We just basked in each other's presence, touching each other with Sight in the lost places we had done without all of our lives up until now. It was a suffering and a salvation ritual between beloved, familiar companions. Normaine came in.

"Go to sleep for a little while," she ordered. I laid down and she threw a red and black blanket over me.

"Come on, Mama of 'Girl Who Needs to Sleep,' it's time to make spaghetti again!"

These two Shaman women knew what was needed. I helped them make spaghetti before, when one or the other of them was lost somewhere inside themselves. Now they were making spaghetti for me. It was my turn. I hoped they made a ton of it—

enough to fill every bowl in the store. I hoped Cowboy Johnson would fry up Spam too. I pictured the huge stack of fried Spam sandwiches I had first seen repining on a platter in this same room so many years ago. For the first in years, I was as content as a kitten sunning on a warm windowsill. I fell asleep to the sounds of clattering pots and Normaine exclaiming softly, but with much feeling, "Dumbass!" every so often.

They fed me and dressed me as though I was a child. I slept on Cowboy Johnson's cot and on the Hideous Green Sofa in his living quarters. Our living quarters for now. God knows where he stayed. I didn't ask. Normaine and Mama slept near me on one of the many air mattresses the store accumulated over time. Cowboy Johnson made a campfire every night. I helped him. I needed the fire. I stared into the flames and the anguish in my soul slowly burned away.

He told me stories while we watched the flames burn down. Sometimes he quoted famous authors, reading their words by firelight, wearing his black rimmed glasses. Both Mama and Cowboy Johnson liked to tell bird stories.

One night at the campfire Cowboy John asked me, " Wanna' hear the story of Billy Silly Beak, Pearl the Purple Eared Penguin Girl, the Changing Wind, and the Zamboni Ice Floe Man?"

"That's a long assed title," I remarked.

"Yep. It is. Wanna' hear it?"

"Yep."

"Now this story didn't take place around here."

He stirred the fire with his drawing stick.

"It couldn't, because this place is a desert. I don't know if anybody has noticed, but it is full of color and empty space, cactus, road runners, lizards and such. Nothing living here could ever live in that cold northern land where this sad, pitiful little story took place."

He shook his head sorrowfully.

"Yep. This sad tale happened in a cold, black and white place, far north of here. A place where the snow blows nine or ten months out of the year and ice instead of Earth, is the foundation for the few creatures who can stand to live there. The reason I'm telling it tonight is because it is a hot night, and this is a good story to cool down to.

Now, in this cold, bleak country of all black and white, there lived a small penguin named Billy Silly Beak. He lived in an igloo with his parents and an only sister named Merry. M-e-r-r-y Christmas. Their last name was B-e-a-k."

He spelled the name out for us.

"Merry Christmas Beak smiled all the time because she was born on Christmas day, so their parents, Goody Silly Beak and Batty Silly Beak, thought she was a Holy Bird. They believed this because they were of a deeply religious persuasion. Goody Beak's father, Raven Black, was an Episcopalian Minister turned Baptist Missionary, who traveled around their frigid country holding igloo revivals. Nothing like a captive audience. Everywhere he landed was temporary, because he kept melting the ice under the igloos from his long-winded sermons on hell and his wife's culinary disciplines with no kitchen counterintelligence to combat it.

Maybe it was just an indigestion problem, maybe it was more. Who knew?

Batty Silly Beak's parents, Bertha and Bertie Silly Beak once traveled north on an unplanned vacation. Impulsive and heavily feathered, they were shunned by their bird families who believed excessive bird sweat was unmannerly, so they sent them north to cool off and to seek their fortune in a colder climate where scents were not of the essence."

He waited patiently while I groaned loudly and snickered at his choice of words.

"When they landed in the coldest north country of all black and white, Batty Silly Beak, son of Bertha and Bertie, saw Goody Black for the first time. It was love at first flight. Batty Silly Beak soon joined Raven Black's church to court Goody Black. Soon they built an igloo together, and along came their offspring, Billy Silly Beak, then Merry Christmas Silly Beak, the Holy Bird. Merry Christmas Silly Beak naturally became the center of attention. Billy Silly Beak had to take a backseat to his sister in general, and in particular, at Christmas.

Now, Billy Silly Beak yearned with all of his heart for someone to think of him as an important bird. Not necessarily a famous bird, although that would be nice, but someone who would listen to him and understand the true meaning behind his words. He wanted someone who met his high standards. Someone financially stable and predictable. Someone who was a vegetarian, because he heard that vegetarian females were less aggressive than meat eating females. He wanted someone to hang on his every word, to listen to him all day long, and behave as he thought socially appropriate.

In short, he intended to be the Boss. To rule the roost, or should we say igloo? To break the ice, to lead the way across ice floes. He expected to be the whole Boss, and nothing but the Boss of a fine, upstanding female bird, who should be good looking too. Especially in the slim department. Her life would be lived in service to him.

Now Billy Silly Beak didn't realize his ego was as vast as the cold wasteland he lived in, and the daily religious dosage necessary to back it up was conveniently close. But then, every male bird in his village suffered from the same vast ego problem and didn't know it.

Part of the problem was that the Wind blew all the time, bringing change and challenges and news and all kinds of messages like always. Highly irritating to birds determined to hold their silly, chilly positions in place. The Wind tends to ruffle feathers you know.

But the male village birds designed designer earmuffs, branded and labeled them, and stopped listening to the Wind. They did not like being forced into anything, especially change.

Pearl, the Purple Eared Bird Girl, never wore wear earmuffs, hence her purple ears. She liked listening to the Wind. She stayed familiar with the Wind's voices and what they said. Pearl told the rest of the inhabitants of the village the things the Wind said, but they turned away. They turned away because she wasn't religiously reliable or financially stable. Or skinny. Pearl was tall with many curves, a mind of her own, a large, soft bosom that many a bird model in L.A. once envied. Yes, she'd been there too. It was whispered that Pearl was the result of a liaison between an island parrot named Joe and her mother, a famous botanist and world traveler. The bottom line was, she wasn't one of them. And worse, she didn't want to be.

Now it just so happened that Billy Silly Beak became enamored of Pearl, but he didn't want to be, or understand why. He ran away and sat on the same small ice floe each time he yearned to be with her, and the Wind, being helpful and much wiser than either of them, blew his ice floe farther and farther away from her. Each time he found himself by her side, smiling at her or reaching out to smooth her feathers, he rushed back to his ice floe and the Wind blew him out of reach of Pearl.

He told himself Pearl wasn't for him. He deserved better, and he knew it. After all, he was a most charismatic and handsome little bird with the true glass grey eyes of a color seldom seen in this north country, and a dimple in his chin like Kirk Penguin the movie star had. He nobly admitted to himself that he was a just a little haughty because he was so handsome and smart.

He stayed comfortable in his world of black and white for a long time. He chose other girlfriends that satisfied his criteria, although they bored him with their judgments, limitations, and unimaginative cooking. He had yet to learn that with the approved package there is always a price to be paid, and one was lucky if it was only insomnia or indigestion.

Becoming both more forbidding and compassionate as he matured, his satisfactory intellectual progress was constantly interrupted by the color of Pearls ears. They were the only color in the black and white landscape they lived in.

Pearl used her large her purple ears to listen to the Wind's stories about tropical islands, and it became essential to her soul that once in a while she hang upside down from the thin ice bridges between ice floes and scream. The Wind informed Pearl that parrots of her ilk live to be hundreds of years old. Pearl didn't know how old she was, but she knew she was older than anyone in the little village.

Billy Silly Beak was afraid of Pearl because she was a wise older bird woman, and her need to scream every now and then clinched it. Billy's nards shriveled up and searched for new, higher hiding places each time he heard Pearl scream. But Pearl had no calling to become a nun, you see, she was madly in love with Billy Silly Beak.

Well, it just didn't work out. So, they both mated with other birds, reared offspring and grew old, and their children moved away, and time went on, and they each lost their spouses. They were alone once more, and Pearl's purple ears became the only color in the landscape for Billy Silly Beak once again. She let him admire her ears and didn't tell him that she wore hearing aids now. When she got close, Billy Silly Beak ran to his trusty little ice floe, and the Wind came and blew him further and further away while he stared at Pearl and Pearl watched him float away.

One day, when there wasn't an icicle to be found hanging from the edges of the Strutting Swoopers whiskers, which tinkled glassily to warn the seals where they were, Billy changed his mind.

He didn't want to run away anymore. He held on to the ice floe and pulled it back to where Pearl stood on the mainland. The Wind tried over and over to blow them apart, but it couldn't. The Wind, like everything else, sometimes wanted things to stay the same as they were. Not often, but sometimes. But Billy Silly Beak was stubborn, if nothing else. Stubbornness was one of his best spiritual attributes. That, and being short sighted. Pearl and Billy Silly beak stayed close and stared at each other. Billy dug deep holes in his little ice floe and held on to the mainland with all his might and stared at Pearl.

The Wind couldn't make Billy Silly Beak let go, so it flew away on an emergency visit to Moody M. (Macaroni) Zamboni, of the Zamboni Ice Floe family. Moody was the son of I. C. and Flo Zen Zamboni. The Wind had a plan. It asked Moody M. Zamboni to flood Billy's ice floe with a thin stream of hot water so the floe would freeze smooth and slick, therefore, causing Billy Silly Beak to have no place to hold on to. Then the Wind could blow him away from Pearl again. That was the plan.

The Wind waited in the distance, howling and yowling while Moody M. Zamboni the Ice Floe Man, squirted hot water over Billy Silly Beak's little ice floe. Billy Silly Beak solved the problem quickly. He simply stepped onto a different ice floe. The Moody M. (Macaroni) Zamboni, the ice Floe Man, squirted hot water on all of the ice floes near Billy Silly Beak, making all of them slick as glass.

He didn't know Billy Silly Beak now knew he could no longer retreat to an ice floe when things got too warm with Pearl. He would have just have to stay with her on the mainland and sweat it out. Finally, the Wind gave up and left. Moody M. (Macaroni) Zamboni went back home carrying a hastily built snow crush snowman as a present for his parents, the venerable I. C. and Flo Zen Zamboni.

So, the two of them, Billy and Pearl, began standing side by side, close together at the water's edge for hours at a time, watching waves and learning each other's rhythms. Then one night when the black sky was filled with white stars, the two of them were seen entering a new igloo together while Billy Silly Beak's cousin, Belvis Harry Sideburn Beak, a master musician of many talents, tweeted, warbled, and chirped outside.

Were they happy? Did they and the Wind and Moody, the Zamboni Ice Floe Man have any more adventures together?

Would Billy Silly Beak become legendary for being the handsomest, most debonair old penguin in town someday?

Would Pearl remain enamored of him after she got to know him?

Would they weather the long winter blizzard ahead together?

They were too old to do like the younger penguins and spend their time producing offspring. Would they find a seniors penguin club and take tours on ships filled with icy handed massage therapists, fishy chefs, or spend their spare time learning to dance the Skaters Tango or making ice sculptures?

And Moody, the Zamboni Ice Floe Man...where was he when you needed him to slick and slide things up? Legend has it that he is still laying down layers of ice here and there in the somber, frozen black and white north, and any little wakeful, troublesome penguins are warned that Moody M. (Macaroni) Zamboni the Ice Floe Man, might find them and freeze their feet forever to an ice floe that the Wind will blow away to somewhere else if they don't go to sleep quickly at night. I personally think Moody M. is in Atlantic City gambling again; but what do I know? So now this bitter, cold little story has been told."

I never discovered any glaring, specific moral to his stories, but they were comforting and true. I thought about life and how we are layered with stories, all kinds of emotions, a short amount of time, and great intentions. We are swept up in the winds of Being, of Knowing, and Seeing. Time is. Time was. Time passes.

Lovers have their own language. Ray and I used to have our own language. I remembered the subtle changes in him when he came home from college each time. And suddenly I knew there were others back then. Almost idly, without feeling, I wondered what happened to them. Did they almost lose themselves like me when they realized he would never theirs?

Cowboy Johnson told Celia stories, too. Her favorite one was Chirpy and Cheep Cheep. He told it with variations each time.

"Chirpy and Cheep Cheep were both very front porch birds. They loved to fly around their neighborhood all day long, watching other birds and people and their dogs and cats and what they were doing. They followed the mailman when he whistled. They landed delicately and daintily ate a few seeds from Mrs. Prattlehouse's red bird feeder and preened for her each morning while she waved at them through her living room window.

They didn't fly to back windows; all that was back there were cats trying to sneak up on them, or odiferous containers awaiting the refinements of emptiness. In practical terms, that means being less smelly. At that point, Chirpy flew north, and Cheep Cheep flew south, searching out new happenings. Some days, they flew east and west. But at the end of the day, they sat together on the shady lower limbs under the tree house they lived in and discussed what each one saw that day.

But after Chirpy left Mrs. Prattlehouse's bird feeder one ordinary day, he stayed gone all afternoon and came home, a changed bird. How was he changed? He couldn't hide his change, and maybe he didn't want to. Nobody knows the answer to that Why, since his change was obvious to the whole world!

That's because Chirpy came home with a rather large mouthful of false teeth. One might even say huge. His big new teeth forced him to smile at everybody and everything in sight, and to become a devoted carnivore. He had no chance of ever being a moody little bird who cried or yelled or chirped much even. Every time he tried to get bitter about no worms or too many leaves falling, his new false teeth swept his face up into a smile. They forced him to smile. Even when he slept. He had to take up gargling each morning before he chirped. Otherwise, it was just a dry, nothing chirp.

Cheep Cheep, who always emulated Chirpy, asked him where he had been.

"I flew over the hills of Montana, down the same trail Johnny Appleseed followed, and back out into the plains of Sand Hill crane country, where the egrets beak you if you don't move on fast enough. Then I flew through the flamingo pinks of a thousand voices of glorious sopranos singing in high C, and somehow, due to my usual impeccable, terrifying, horrifying bad timing, I landed in front of a dentist's office in Detroit."

Cheep Cheep thought this was taking the long way home, but wisely, did not impede Chirpy's narrative with a comment.

"The dentist's office was next to a pet store. By this time, I was exhausted, so I perched on what I thought was a rug.

Chirpy gave him a huge smile and shrugged.

"Hey, it was soft. I fell asleep and dropped off of it when it started moving, and whatever it was, used its paw to kicked me through the dentist's office door. The door was propped open because of frequent inclement interior odors emanating. Now this was an animal dentist's office. That was why it was next to the pet shop. Convenience, you know?"

"Someone said, "Here, fill out these papers." So I did. They found out that I wasn't incontinent, had a strong warble in my throat, liked grits, and lived on the lower limb of a tree house.

They were impressed by where I lived, my address as it were, and decided for job security reasons, that I should be able to smile at anyone who came to visit the tree house. So, they put me under and gave me the super deluxe false teeth model.

Trouble is, the dentures keep hopping out and running away. Sadly, I now own run-away dentures on a payment plan. But they are not happy. They say they are too big for my mouth, and they are tired of being squeezed in. They complain that I am not providing a big enough mouth for their living quarters and are making plans to sue me. What can I do?

I know they are planning to run away again. I can tell. When I take them out at night, they go off and whisper together. I'm turning into a paranoid bird. Maybe I will even become a mute bird, if this keeps up.

Also, being a carnivore is not as easy as it was before I got my dentures. I used to have a yearning for worms of all kinds and a yen for bugs. But now I dream of bigger prey. Or at least the dentures do."

It didn't take long before word got around, and many others visited the tree house to see Chirpy and his teeth. But sadly, though he tried, Chirpy never got the big head. So, the teeth packed their toothpaste, toothbrushes and floss and ran away one night after Chirpy settled in for the night.

Nobody wanted to see an ordinary bird with stretch marks around his beak, and too much gas in the infernal regions, so everybody stopped coming to the tree house to see Chirpy.

In the end, Chirpy and Cheep Cheep, who still thought Chirpy was the cat's meow, figuratively speaking, settled back into their old life and its routines, and lived happily ever after on the lower branches of the tree house far, far away from Montana."

I listened to his wonderful stories, ate miles of spaghetti with various sauces, including barbeque, and accepted all the advice and caring my family of misfits gave me. I slowly got better.

Each day I walked up and down the road and in the desert behind the store. The desert was spotted like a beautiful leopard, tattooed with patterns of lizards and patterns of creations made before time began. Harmony surrounded me. Nothing was insignificant, and slowly my soul expanded in joy.

A bobcat started showing itself to me sometimes. I was scared of it and asked Normaine to go with me on my walks. She watched it and assured me that it was one of my totem animals there to help me, not to harm me.

"What does a bobcat following me mean, Normaine?" I asked. She frowned and studied the ground before she answered.

"Hear this, Dumbass, and hear it good 'cause I won't tell it again. Not to anyone. The bobcat is small and fierce, and not to be messed with, or it can tear your ass up. You, like your Mama, take it for granted that all feelings are large and looming and cast a huge Shadow. But that's bull crap. Some feelings are small and fierce like the bobcat, and they will tear your ass up if you try to mess with them by trying to get rid of them or trying to "fix" them.

Nature ain't sorry for what it is, so stop trying to apologize to it for what you are. It don't understand apologies., Dumbass! There's small, medium, and large in everything including the Creator. What makes you think feelings are exempt from that, Boohoo Baby?"

She rubbed her hands together in anticipation.

"Now let's talk about doing the wild thing! Everything in Nature does it. It's only natural."

She shrugged. I stayed for her lecture. I didn't run away this time.

"Some have fun with it, some don't. I got the worst of it over with first in the beginning, now I got the best of it. You ain't hardly got started on what good poontang and what sweatin' it out under a fine, fun lovin' man means!"

"Shut up, Normaine!"

I couldn't take any more. I laughed and shouted at her and ran for Washman's Draw. I thought about beautiful, charming, inflexible, rigid, cold Ray. Would he be a different kind of lover if he was warm and kind and funny? I never thought about personality and the wild thing and how they went together before.

I reached Washman's Draw and stopped, remembering Ray's proposal to me. He had kneeled in this same red dirt, his black hair shining, him so beautiful in the sun, and me more powerful and beautiful than I had ever been, or ever would be again, most likely.

Normaine appeared, panting. I studied her. Her black hair was wet, and she was bent over, one eye looking out at the desert, the other eye looking at me. She looked like she did the day I met her. I studied her while she caught her breath. After a while I said, "You have a terrible beauty, Normaine."

I meant it, too. She finally got her breath back and straightened up.

"When I was in the pen, they operated on me for appendicitis, and took that opportunity to fix me because I was an Indian."

"What?"

"You know. Spayed? Neutered? No more bird nest?"

The world rocked beneath my feet as I took in the implications of it. Her son was the only child she would ever have, and he was lost to her. And here I was whining to myself about Ray and Celia. I should tell her.

"I had such a hard time having Celia that there can't be any more. Don't tell Mama or anybody, okay?"

We stared at each other with the ancient knowledge of the women's wisdom we each carried. Only women held the wombs birthing human life onto Earth. Some people liked this, and some didn't, so there were countless things that could and did happen to women's wombs and the birthing process. Time passed and the wind blew. After a long time, I went to her and put my arm across her shoulder and turned her toward home.

"I guess we'll just have to share Celia."

I thought of something else and added, "Until you and your son can be together again. That's not so long now."

Chapter Eighteen

I don' knows 'bout other lost folks,
but when I's bad lost, I jist' look a' round fer' de'
signs
showin' me the right way ta' go,
jis' like any other smart fool would do,
cause da' signs eba' where fo' eba' body
da' Lord doan' miss a' one once't I fin' dat' sign,
den' I walk my skinny ass and bony ankles on down
da' line.
uh huh!

One day I was wandering out in the desert a mile
or so behind the motel when I noticed a flock of white
birds flying high above me. They were flying in
purposeful formation, a high, white arrow pointing
north. Normaine told me north was the home of the
ancients, and if I ever saw any signs pointing in that
direction, to be very, very careful.

I peered up at the birds. They looked delicate and
snowy white with long legs, like egrets. I thought I
knew all the bird types living around here from my
school studies, but I didn't know this type, or why
any birds resembling the crane family might be flying
over a desert in the summer.

"They want you to remember the snow," Normaine
whispered in my ear.

Suddenly, my heart leapt with joy. I held out my
arms and twirled in the warm sand and hugged her,
though I didn't have a clue what she meant.

I never did ask, for with her words, the communion with the algebraic divinity within me finally started up again. The key was somehow turned; the engine was revving. I felt profound at not being lost any more. My angels, guides, and beings were with me again. We could pursue math together again. I searched me internally and it looked like my psychic abilities were intact. Where I was headed and what I would do started all over again. A new lease on life. I was in recovery.

Animals came to me four times that summer, each from a different direction. Each one lifted me into a new place. After I saw the white birds, I dreamed of snow. The snow taught me how to be in a relationship with cold and white.

I dreamed of being lost without fear in a blizzard, of sleeping in an igloo, and of watching snow fall outside a picture window while standing inside a warm house holding a cup of steaming hot cocoa. I dreamed I slept in tiny, cozy rooms as an old, wrinkled person-Rip Van Winkle-, while the snow and wind piled snow drifts against the doors and windows. I swam beneath northern ice floes in pale green water beside a giant, patient whale who activated the hormones I dammed up as a child and adolescent by shoving me gently side to side. I stood small in frozen northern lands beneath tall trees hundreds of years old, and watched the tradition keeping, sober winter northern Elemental Elders standing as tall as the sky. Life was solemn to them. There was no laughter and dancing in their Elemental realms. They ruled stillness and all that it allowed. Their speech was harsh, their expressions forbidding, their space completely theirs to rule, down to the last detail.

After a time, I intuited that the Northern Elders kept the lands of Chaos and the homes of Not Knowing bordered and apart. Not Knowing and Chaos were active forces taking place constantly throughout the universe. Winter maintains a covenant with the Creator to keep them eternally boundarized by moving them into stillness when needed

Like a Mandelbrot set, the universe is constantly organizing itself, causing chaos to become self-organizing so new chaos can begin. The giant Winter Elders transformed Chaos and Not Knowing, then set them free through warmth to self-organize. Cold, then warm, then back into hot chaos again.

Ray had led me into the chaos of not knowing and left me there without a coat or a blanket. How was I to get out of this blizzard with no name, the snow that covered all with stillness, the silence holding no answers in the frozen darkness of an unending night? In my dream time, I realized I would never find those answers. Others, yes. But not those.

They were not to be known. Those answers were for another day, another time, another lifetime far beyond this one. I was to accept what was, walk out of the snow, out of my chaos and misery, let Spirit rule the world again, and get on with this lifetime.

Each day, In the early morning hours, I relaxed in a new way. Spirit took me in its arms and cradled me. I fell into deep, peaceful sleeps, ones I needed and was deprived of since childhood.

A new awakening began. I slept here and there and everywhere with unrestrained freedom, deeply resting, and from what I was told, snoring with abandon. I told them I wasn't snoring. I was just practicing riding a motorcycle in my dreams.

They laughed and shook their heads, pleased that I was joking. I started my sleeping around on the Hideous Green Sofa, but I didn't stop there. I snuggled up to Normaine on the air mattress. From there, I took over Cowboy Johnson's cot. I took naps, too. Good sweet, long naps. Good, sweet sleep. On the porches, everywhere.

*

One day I was sitting on a stump resting my face in my hands, contentedly dozing off out at the campfire, when a lizard ran across my ankle, startling me awake. Bold little thing. I looked down at the lizard. It was about five inches long, with red markings like tiny flames running along its tan sides. I laughed. The absurd little thing looked just like a miniature four-cylinder Healy Silverstone race car from the forties with flames painted on its sides.

The little lizard ran off, stopped a dozen feet away, and looked back at me. Its spiny tail left ridge marks behind it in the sand. I watched it blink its eyes a couple of times before it moved another ten feet away, stood up and started dancing. What the hell! I never saw anything like it! I was staring at the lizard in a fascinated stupor when Normaine whispered in my ear.

"The south is calling you now. Everything romantic in life is so because of hot, sweet Mother Nature."

She strolled away, smirking. I watched as another Healy Silverstone lizard, tan and smaller, with demure yellow flames painted on its sides, rushed up to the larger, waiting lizard. They stood up and began to dance and then to copulate madly with complete abandon in a ritual as old as time. Their innocence reminded me of Ray and I and the heated love and passion we shared in the beginning. Once upon a time, we danced and flamed hot for each other like these lizards in a hot summer long ago, under the sun. There were many of those times. And we still went south to the Bahamas in our big old bed every now and then. But it was just for a brief vacation, not a place we lived in any more.

I suppose that is the way of things for humans. With that thought, something inside me cooled down and dropped away. The lizards ran off. I stared out at the empty desert. I needed to give up trying to build a home on a tropical island, a never never land where I would always be happy, a place where Ray would be happy, and Celia a perfect child. It was much too hot to live there all the time.

I sensed the new, empty place waiting for me now, one that would cost me, but one I could reside in with dignity and joy. It would have to be a second home, a home that fit inside the walls of the big house in Carolina, a big home already holding acceptance of love and laughter and tears and secret disappointments. It must be a home where we could mine the gold from the dark fires burning in each of us. Some fires were old, some were new. but we all had them. The language of the soul, heat, fire, anger, and all of the passions, spoke through the inner voices of intuition and path finding, and they were working in me right now, arranging and rearranging my innards.

"Geena come sit on the porch. It's too hot out here for you. Let's get you into some shade." Mama's calm voice interrupted my thoughts. I stood up and let her guide me away from the campfire and up the steps to the back porch.

*

Another day at dusk, I was sitting on the front porch holding an orange. I planned to peel it, then break it up into sections and eat it. The orange was golden and luscious and juicy. It smelled as though it was just picked off a life filled, beautiful orange tree.

I watched idly as a raven flew in from the west, followed by a dozen or more ravens. The raven leader lit on the railing and cawed an order at me at me in a raucous, raspy voice. A couple of the raven's fellow travelers lit near the steps in the yellow desert dust. The rest lit by the gas pumps, their beady black eyes staring avidly at the orange in my hand.

Suddenly, I wanted to eat that orange more than anything else in the world. All of it. I didn't want to share even one tiny morsel of its juicy goodness. I hefted it in my hand. It felt full and plump. Maybe, just maybe, it was full of the unknown fulfillment I was yearning for. Stories of princesses and ugly green frogs and glowing, magic golden balls buried beneath the earth at dusk ran through my mind. Maybe it was the last orange in the world.

I eyed the raven leader that cawed at me. I knew about Raven. Raven was a Trickster. Tricksters were old magicians. They developed their ways long ago to survive. Tricksters made life into an art form, a beautiful, dark game filled with shocks and shudders, yet the most intense of joys, especially when it came to copulating. One took their chances with Tricksters, for they mostly tricked people and got away with it. I decided to be cautious.

What caused this flock of ravens to stop at a store out in the middle of the desert? I hefted the orange again. I wasn't going to give up my magic golden ball to the flighty, noisy tricksters waiting before me. Why should I?

Suddenly, a vision of the ravens flashed into my mind. They were judges dressed in black robes waiting to indict me for something I didn't know anything about.

People led dangerous, painfully unconscious lives because they were always doing things without knowing why. Maybe they committed dastardly deeds in past lives. That damned karma again. Mama once explained it to me. She said the third eye slowly opened through expansion of our conscious awareness. The operative word was slowly, for one saw both the beautiful, the painful, and the ugly in equal amounts. They were attached to each other and in balance. Never one without the other. That was the law. The third eye should be opened slowly, so our souls could stand both the pain and beauty of the human condition. Otherwise, it would destroy us.

With those black, beady raven eyes confronting me, I was forced to admit a part of me that fled from my childhood Shadow while riding in the back seat of Mama's 57 Mercury all of those years ago, had stayed in that same back seat, and never opened the door and got out again. That part liked it there. Ii didn't know if it could survive experiencing any more of what men and women did to each other in the name of love. That's why it wouldn't get out of the Merc'.

Now I was being forced to get out of the Merc'. Because of me and Ray. That's what it came down to. It was time to look at what was between us, including the sex part, or die a slow painful, psychic death in the backseat of a hot, old land yacht. Or a cold one, depending on the weather.

Ray was my only lover and I purposefully kept my knowledge narrowed to what was between us. The coldness of who he was made it easy to do.

Mama and Cowboy Johnson and I went to Taliesin West a couple of times. I had admired Frank Lloyd Wright's cars there. Now I had to live like Frank Lloyd Wright and his wife Olgivanna and sit in my own 1937 A.C. 16/80 Two Seat Sport Competition Roadster and smile with knowledge and learn the expert handling of much more than cars.

I needed to develop my organic character if I was to gain decent hormones to move on with. I pictured the car that bad assed organic part of me would drive. It would be orange and have flames on it and do two hundred miles an hour on the curves.

I peeled the orange. The juice dripped. I divided the orange into sections, one for each bird. One for each black robed judge sitting out there with its knowing black eyes fixed on me. One for each judge that had flown here to help my living flesh take on the hormones I needed to mature further with. The price of the hormones I needed to flood my system with was more knowledge, and the gaining of the wisdom that heading into age needs. The giving up of using Innocence to stay eternally young and hide behind. It meant staying out of the backseat of Mama's 57 Merc'.

I tossed the first piece of orange to the lead raven waiting on the porch railing. It caught the piece of orange in its beak and flew away. The rest of the ravens waited until I tossed their sections of orange to them. They caught them and flew away, too. The ravens were gone like they were never there.

I looked down at the empty orange peel laying on the porch. Were they actually here? I walked down the steps and searched the dust with my eyes to find their footprints to convince myself their presence was not an illusion. The tiny sharp prints were there. I sighed with relief, trudged up the steps and into the store. Chocolate milk and spaghetti. That's what I needed.

Sometime later, maybe it was days, I went to my worktable in the back corner of the store, took up the clay for the first time, and began to shape snowflakes, raindrops, lizards and ravens from it. I painted the snowflakes white, the raindrops blue, the lizards red, and the ravens black.

Chapter Nineteen

You's as sweet as ol' rock candy
made on a hot June afta' noon
I still smell it lak' it was yestiddy'
But no mo' ya's cain't knock' me down
and step ova' me an' do as ya' pleases
cause' I got's skinny, ass kickin' bony ankles
and I's puttin' my daincin' shoes back on.

Early morning, a couple of weeks later, I was working on a clay lizard at my table in the back of the store. Just as the dawn's light made its way into the store, a man opened the front door and walked in. I looked up, startled. The door was supposed to be locked every night. Somebody forgot.

The man was slim and wiry, about five feet eight. He walked with ease down the long length of the store. His smooth gait easily ate up the space between us. I snapped off the small light by my elbow I used to examine my work with and sat the clay lizard down so I could watch him. His boots made hard, clomping sounds on the wood floor.

"Shhhh!" I warned him. He changed his gait immediately and tiptoed over to my workplace.

"They are still sleeping. Somebody forgot to lock the front door. What do you want?"

"Just some gas for my old blue Nash Rambler, and a Coke or coffee if you have it."

I yawned mightily.

"Okay," I sighed.

"I guess the day has started."

Then I realized what he just said.

"You're driving a Nash Rambler?"

He smiled a slow, wicked smile.

"Yep."

"What year?"

"A 1951. But Adam has seen better days," he said ruefully. We tiptoed out the front door and made our way down the steps and over to the beat up old blue Nash sitting by the gas pumps. I used the key to free up a gas nozzle, and the man started pumping gas. I looked him up and down. He was wearing blue jeans and a blue tee shirt.

And he had a blue Nash.

"You like blue," I surmised out loud.

"Yeah. How did you guess?"

He smiled a slow, easy smile, and looked me full in the eyes. I stared back examining his eyes. They were a light sky blue, a beautiful, perfect sky bird blue inside, ringed with a darker blue outside, as blue as rainwater reflected in a wood barrel setting out under the hot desert sun. I watched gold flecks mix and dance with the light blue water. I moved on to his lashes and hair. They were shades of light brown mixed with reds and golds, like my hair. He was fair skinned with a young face lined and weathered by freckles and deep thoughts. He watched me respectfully, but I knew instinctively that this man could look clear through me if he wanted to. He was psychic, too. My first male psychic. I relaxed.

"I'm as far away from all of this as a body can be," I muttered to him and myself in an impulsive, long lived desperation I didn't understand the need of.

"I'm so damned tired of it."

He nodded.

"Me, too. That's why I'm on the road."

His voice was warm and smooth with no gravel in it. We stared searchingly at each other for minute, then we pulled it back. There would be no story shared here, whining and piteous though it might be. When he was done, we slipped back into the store. I handed him a Coke, and he paid me for the gas and the Coke.

"I'll need a room too, for a couple of days if you have one. Until I can get Adam back on his feet."

"Adam the Nash" I stated.

"Yes. He needs a little tune up, and I see you have a garage beside the store. I can do the work, but the garage would be convenient."

I spoke briskly to hide the surge of ridiculous joy I felt at his announcement.

"Motel room number three. It's all decorated in blue. I did the decorating. Here is your key. Everybody pays up front."

He paid. I handed him a key from the wood board behind the counter.

"Enjoy your stay. The store, motel, and garage open at eight."

He swooped up the Coke, nodded, and turned away. I watched him tiptoe out the door and close it quietly behind him. I was sleepy. I went back to bed and slept like a rock until ten o'clock. By the time I woke up and dressed, Adam the Nash was in the garage being worked on.

"Joe. Joe Waters. That's his name," Cowboy Johnson told me when he came into the store for something.

"Waters."

"Yes," he said and left.

I pondered the name. Was Joe Waters name indicative of the fourth direction, the east? Had the stranger come to advise me on how to begin again? Wasn't that what the east was for? New beginnings? The place of babies and blood and warmth and water? I grabbed a soda and ran down the porch steps into the garage. The two men were looking under the hood of the old blue Nash Rambler.

I yearned to work on the Nash with them, but common sense and the need to be girly won out. The men glanced at me and waited. I minced purposefully over to a folded lawn chair in the corner, dragged it out, opened it, and parked myself in it. Then I started talking. I began with the first birthday I remembered. The men went back to work, murmuring as they consulted about what Adam needed.

"I'll go order the part," Cowboy Johnson said, about an hour later. He left. Joe Waters kept on working on Adam. I was up to three years old in my harrowing life when he interrupted me.

"I have to use the bathroom. Be right back."

He left.

I waited patiently. When he came back, I started talking again. I paced and sat and stood up and started all over again with pacing. I talked until my mouth was dry and my voice raspy. My soda was gone, so I grabbed Joe's Coke, drank it down and talked some more.

Cowboy Johnson came and went without comment. He brought Cokes and sandwiches when I was at ten years old in my telling, and a water hose and soap for washing Adam when I was eleven.

I watched Joe wash Adam tenderly and carefully, and I cried. Then he dried Adam. By the time I was twelve and thirteen, Joe was waxing Adam. By the time he was done, two more hours were gone. Ray and I were married and living in Carolina. By three, Celia was born, and we were on our way to the store. By four, I had described my slough of despond over Ray, and my sad life of imperfections.

"Now you know all about me," I concluded. I felt wonderful. Thin and light and pretty, with an inner emptiness full of the promise of bold adventures in my future. Reborn. I almost talked this man to death, and he somehow survived the onslaught of my verbiage. He deserved a medal. A stranger in blue named Joe Waters, who drove an old blue Nash Rambler.

"Thank you Joe Waters."

I spoke from the depths of my soul. Cowboy Johnson came in and headed off my need to genuflect before the stranger.

"Time for dinner. It's spaghetti time once again," he said dryly, leaving me to figure it out.

"You're welcome to eat with us, Joe."

"I think I'll take rain check," Joe said hastily. "I'll just grab a soda and sandwich or something from the store."

I let Cowboy Johnson take my hand and lead me away. He led me to the table in the back room where Normaine slapped a plate full of spaghetti down in front of me and snickered.

"Well, Gabby Gus is eating with us."

I flipped my hair to the side instead of answering. I examined it and noticed it was past my waist again, and bore a slight green tinge to it. I liked it.

I applied myself to the spaghetti. Nothing she could say could bother me. I felt beautiful and whole, empty of trash, and glowing. After I ate, I went to bed. The rest of them went to the camp fire. Celia was out at her grandmother Emma's, and all was well.

I woke up the next morning knowing I was a nomad once again. My status as a world traveler interested in wheels of life, and all of the other arts my willful soul might turn to was back. Blue days at sea lay ahead. I sat up and yawned. Where was that man? My water man. I wanted to jump his bones. Sleep with him. Find a place to get naked and laugh with him, touch him, feel the life heat in him. I had never felt the urge to bed with anyone but Ray before. What was going on? I didn't care. I was damn tired of analyzing myself.

I jumped out of bed. I needed to know where he was. I ran out the front door, down the steps and skidded to a stop. Joe Waters was working under the hood of Adam with Cowboy Johnson standing beside of him. They both glanced at me and went back to their discussion.

I ran back up the steps and into the store. I was still in my pajamas. I changed clothes hastily, searching for the sexiest clothes I owned. Thanks to Normaine, I owned something besides black to wear. I dug out a simple, red silk, short sleeved shirt and a pair of black Capri pants. I pulled them on, washed my face, sat down and brushed my long hair. I brushed until the tangles were gone and tied it back into a smooth, shiny brown pony tail. I found a pair of tan sandals, but hesitated. Would I be cuter going barefoot as usual, or wearing them? Barefoot. Definitely. I applied a thick layer of red lipstick and rushed back to the garage.

Cowboy Johnson turned and looked at me and did a double take. Joe kept on working. I waited until he turned around. Then I posed and simpered. Joe Waters and I stared at each other for a long time. Finally, Cowboy Johnson gave up.

"You need a keeper, Geena, but it isn't going to be me."

He shook his head and walked out. I rushed close to Joe and looked him in the eyes.

"We've just got a minute. Cowboy Johnson will tell somebody on me, and they'll be out here in a minute."

I touched his sleeve while he watched me with steady, calm eyes.

"I can pick you up later tonight..." I blushed... "...behind your room?...maybe?"...since Adam isn't running right now?.. we can go... driving?"

We were close to the same height. I waited and looked straight into his eyes. He nodded just as Normaine strolled into the garage.

"I need a lug nut wrench for Eddy."

Her sparkling eyes traveled back and forth between the two of us. I went back in the store and worked on clay. The night couldn't come soon enough for me. I wandered through the day feeling guilty about Ray, and what I was planning to do with another man. Celia was still with her Grandmother Emma out at the ranch.

All I could think about was the terrible hunger that stirred up in me when I met Joe. A hunger for a slow, gentle touch, for praise, kind words for who I am, a little admiration and honesty. Sweetness. I wanted more than anything in the world to lay my head on his shoulder and rest it there. Maybe throughout eternity. I didn't know what would be enough. And I didn't care whether he wanted or needed me back.

That thought would have appalled me not more than a day ago, but I had entered into the world of needy harlotry. I was beginning to understand harlotry as being a very different thing when you have never been in it. Being a woman condemned and misunderstood by both men and women for her actions because of her need for a man.

I took down my ponytail, shook my hair out, put on a fire engine red blouse and tight stretchy pants. I did a sneaky drive by and picked him up in "Gracie", my 1959 Dodge, plush and lush and spacious, a perfect pimpmobile, just in case, after the camp fire turned to ashes and everyone else was in bed.

We spun through the still night under the stars in the dying warmth of the desert darkness. He slid close to me as though he knew I needed his nearness and warmth. I could smell his aftershave, and after a while, he kissed me on the neck and ran his hands through my hair. I pulled into Washman's Draw and stopped. I left the headlights on and searched until I found a radio station playing slow waltz music.

"I'm just a hippie guy but I love making love better than anything." He warned me with his words of what I might expect.

"Have you made love with a lot of women?" I asked this hopefully.

"Yes," he answered after a minute, "I have."

"Do you regret it?"

"No. Not ever."

He waited while I made up my mind.

"Well, then I won't either."

We got out and waltzed in the headlight's glow until Joe took my hand and led me back to Gracie, where he doused the headlights. We undressed in the dark and tossed our clothes through Gracie's window. I took the blanket from the back seat and spread it out on the sand. The air flowed over us, and a million stars watched as we came together and an old questioning hunger in me was at last satisfied. Put to rest. Grateful to the Goodness in this psychic water man, I gave everything I could to him. Caresses and sounds and warm touching. I knew about those things. And it seemed to be enough. Hell, he knew my life story after all my babbling yesterday. Yesterday seemed like ages ago now. It was lived through by a different person. I asked him to tell me about himself, but he said that wasn't part of what was going on. Hours later, I dropped him off a little ways from the store, and he walked back to his room.

The store was dark when I slipped through the back door and made my way past Cowboy Johnson's cot and lay down on the Hideous Green Sofa. I listened to Mama and Normaine's soft snoring as they lay on the air mattresses close to the cot where they had been keeping their vigil over me. Well, they wouldn't have to any longer. I was back. But different. I didn't know what the different part was yet, but I was satisfied with it.

I met Joe Waters three nights in a row. He left on the fourth morning. "Adam" the Nash's new parts were installed, so there was no reason for Joe to linger. He headed east down the two-lane blacktopped highway running its narrow way in front of the store. I waved until I could no longer see him. And that is how I came back to this world to live and love differently in it.

Mama and I moved back into our rooms, and Normaine moved back in with Eddy in their motel room. Not one of them said a word about the three nights I was missing. I yearned for Joe Waters, my psychic water man, my man of the east after he left, but I did not need him or any other man in the same way anymore.

My water man was a sexual healing angel dressed in blue mornings, with eyes reflecting both the stormy sea and the still water mirrored in a rain full barrel resting under the sun. Peace to him and me. What we came together for was our karma. A much-needed gift from the universe. We didn't need to live together or make a long-term commitment to care about each other. We both knew we were in the world together now. We were travelers in this universe, meeting and exchanging gifts, then going on our separate ways, stronger and better than before.

My water man was not afraid of how much I could love, how strongly I felt. He met me in their depths and never ran. I didn't run from my agony and love, and he didn't run for cover. Our lovemaking went where it needed to.

As for me, a part of me grew up those three nights. I did the one thing I believed I could never do. My love was okay. It was not too much, like Ray tried to convince me it was. I learned that not all men harbor lethal genitals and abhor women's strong emotions. I learned this from the water man. I breathed deep now.

Ray's inner coldness gave me a cold, safe, loving relationship. One I could stand. A relationship filled with true heat or passion would have destroyed me before, for I wasn't ready for it. Joe brought my fire and passion to me when I was ready for it.

Soul mates. Different kinds and loves from each of them. Any new men coming into my life would be met with my new foundation of experience and understanding. The wow factor was gone. Now it was about relevant sharing. The struggles and joys of the seasons of my life lay before me, and now I could breathe easier through them, whatever happened. I could breathe again. I was complete.

*

I stopped making birds, snowflakes, lizards, and ravens. I went out to Emma's. She helped me make a small clay bust of Joe. His head was no bigger than a baseball with a flat base. She patiently questioned me about his features and shaped them for me. I told her about him, and realized I had known Joe countless lifetimes. Emma must have seen the love I had for Joe instead of her son, but she never said it.

At last I realized the mistake I was making, hurting her with a chosen other than her son, and we made a bust of Ray together with Celia, and we all three explained a mother's, a child's, and a wife's love for him to each other. It both broke something in us and healed something too.

That was as good as I could do. I took the bust back to the store and mailed it home to Carolina to Ray. When he came home that fall, he placed it center stage in the living room of our house. I stayed strong and full of purpose all summer. My life was back, broken but reorganized, and I planned to live it joyfully.

I was a very passionate woman. The sexual aspects of my passions had flowered safely in two different ways, one under the coolness of Ray's love, the second under the heat of my water man's affection. With Ray, I left my father behind. With Joe Waters, I bloomed joyously into my waiting womanhood at last. I had grown up and was now a woman filled with my own passions and purposes.

"I love Ray. You know I do. I always will."

I told Emma this before we left to go back to Carolina at the end of the summer. We were out at the ranch. Celia was outside playing. Emma searched my face and then met my eyes.

"I know you love him, even though you are not emotionally compatible. Not every relationship you lose is an unexpected loss. Sometimes it is a gain. Who knows? Life has unexpected places it needs to go, sometimes to just help it stay strong," she answered me carefully.

"I won't ever keep Celia away from you, Emma, whether we disagree or not on things. You have my word."

She breathed a sigh of relief. We both understood what she was asking. We were both learning more about the true depth of our humanity and our potential with each other.

I said to her, "I have seen many strange things in my life. Once when I was with Ray in the Amazon, we saw a Caiman lizard with its head covered in butterflies drinking its tears. It's called "lachryphagy". Tear feeding. There was no source of salt for them, and they need salt to live, so they were drinking the tears of the Caiman lizard for the salt in them. I've seen butterflies drinking turtle tears for salt too."

I had no further words to explain the situation with.

Emma studied me again.

"I understand. In the Canary Islands, there is an island where the people don't use the spoken word. Instead, they communicate through the sounds of the Wind. They use various pressures of whistling sounds to communicate. I learned to say 'Come here,' 'Thank you,' and 'That will do, in whistle language. I wonder if they don't communicate more and better than we do?"

She said, "The words chosen or discarded for dictionaries are changing again. The time will come when children are no longer taught the words acorn, dandelion, fern, chipmunk, otter, meadow, and brooks. The words of our old world are rapidly being lost. I see it in the art world all the time." She shrugged.

"We need to save the seeds of our indigenous plants, our words and the old ways. But time has a way of turning them to dust in spite of everything we do to preserve them."

I studied Emma. She was an introvert, one who painted like a bull fighter fought when they were in the ring. Her true makeup was to sit on the sidelines, unseen, yet she painted with the strongest of positive yang energy. The colors poured out onto her canvases. Gorgeous and strong. The best of the color energies mingled in an architecture of wonder for all to see.

People tended to assume that Emma Makepeace was yang, like her artwork—that she liked to be social and laugh a lot and strut around and be a big shot. But she was just the opposite. Being in the limelight, being famous, was a trial and tribulation to her. She was a true introvert, like the Water Whisperers in Belarus in Eastern Europe, who whisper words into water and have the sick drink the water, and it heals them. They heal people and animals and all that come to them for healing. Only, Emma healed through her artwork. When people saw her work, they were thrown instantly into a totally new grasp of what Awe was. That's a spiritual healing experience.

I knew this from personal experience. I was awed into a new revelation of life the first time I saw her paintings in person. Inspiring Awe in people is not an easy task, and it was Emma's life work.

I remembered the first time I walked into her living room, a young girl with long hair past her butt, running from a Monster with the help of a mother who could count stars but not dollars. Such a long time ago!

I blew out a breath as I studied Emma. Pride is a natural attribute of the soul. I'd observed a few other people with Sight besides us. Most of them believed they were too spiritually wise to have to be decent to other people. They became spiritually pompous, narcissists doing a few tours of duty on what they viewed as a ghetto planet. But no one is already there.

I also heard that some aliens have beliefs so far beyond us that our world doesn't make sense to them, so they refuse to land here and hang out with us. Well, neglect is said to be the absence of attention.

Emma wasn't like that. She was tender, hidden, and secretive. Bold and amazing. Truthful and delicate. A lovely, lovely woman.

Emma was studying me back.

"I paint to give myself strength," she said. "I paint to have in my life what I could not otherwise. I paint to be the person I become when I paint. I paint to explore the things I'm afraid of and delighted by. It keeps most people indifferent to my shortcomings." She smiled.

I responded with one of my odd answers. Odd, to me and everybody else. Over the years I was able to curb this propensity, but sometimes it slipped out anyway.

"Did you know that many people die of pneumonia and lung stuff because people can't remember how we breathed from the ancient days when we had gills? People die because they are lying flat on their backs. They can't breathe through their backs. The older people get, the more they need to breathe through their backs. That's why the spine moves forward. To protect and make available more air from the back. The need for air takes priority over the organs. Beds need to have holes in them or be aerated somehow. Basically, people need to sleep up. And stay sitting up when they have lung issues."

Emma was used to me and didn't comment. She waited for the rest. I studied her. There is no level of wisdom so wise it makes love unnecessary.

"Miss Emma, Celia is like you in many ways. She has the Sight, and it looks like it will flow toward you."

She nodded.

"Yes."

I picked up a brush and toyed with it. I examined it intently so I wouldn't have to look at her. "There is only Celia, you know. No more."

After a while she said, "I guessed as much a long time ago."

She didn't say any more. She didn't have to and maybe couldn't.

I said, "Maybe we need to learn to dance at funerals! After all, there was time when women wore wreaths around their heads at weddings! They still do in parts of the Ukraine. Why not wear them for funerals, too?"

My eyes filled with tears. Emma hugged me.

"It will all come out right."

"Or not!" I added. "We are living organics! You and I and Mama are like tree mothers. Underneath trees there is this other world of complex, biological pathways that connect one tree to another, and they are able to communicate through this infinite network as though they are One. And, they recognize their own offspring! Isn't that amazing?"

"Yes, it is. Geena, I want us two to go to the south of France soon. Can we arrange that?"

Before Emma could say any more, Celia came running in, her face rosy with smiles and we put our talk away.

Mama always talked about the Shadow. It turns out there are three parts to a Shadow. Umbra is the Latin word for Shadow. The Umbral Shadow, which is the blackest, darkest part, and the Penumbral Shadow which is the less dark fringe, the gray surrounding the center of the Shadow, then the Antumbra Shadow, which is the Light outlining the Shadow's figure when it is completely contained within the light source.

And so, we create countless shades of white and black and gray as we follow the Path of Totality to its end each time, which ends up in a containment of the Shadow. All Paths of Totality are ruled by the Moon, and all are ten thousand miles long and only one hundred miles wide, so tread carefully, and keep walking. When the Shadow is completely contained within our Light at last, that time still doesn't last long because all things move on, and the Shadow escapes the light again to bring further mysteries for us to discover. It never ends.

Now I can say that I have loved the stars too fondly in this desert place to ever be completely fearful of the night again. This night is here, and those nights were there. And summer will come again to this desert, and to this little white church that was converted into "Cowboy Johnson's Desert Oasis " a long time ago by a bunch of Misfits, and stars twinkling above a woman in love.

Meanwhile, if I ever need to, I can easily find that red cactus desert my real father told me about. And who knows, I might be sitting on the porch in a rocking chair at the store when an old blue Nash Rambler stops for gas again. Time is. Time was. Time is yet to come.

Chapter Twenty

What's a goin' on? Ya' heard what?
dat' ain't so, baby, hell, it's all a lie!
well, if it wadn't, it ain't sa' bad anyhows'
why's you's makin' sa' much of it?
It's jist' a little habit o' mine dat' doan' matta'
anyways, I kin' make it right again
jist' smile at me and say ya' loves me like ya' used to
and we'll jist' start over agin'.

Ray Makepeace

I slammed the phone down in disgust after mother's call. I jumped up and paced the room. Of course, she had to call me on this, the hottest day of summer in Carolina, and pronounce "Ray!" in a grim voice before she informed me of her latest bad news. I have a son. Well, hell! Rayfield Mott Webb. That's the kids name. Nobody knew about him. Except for Rose. All that time since I fooled around with her. Years ago. I'd forgotten all about her.

We were setting new heat records. I wiped my neck with my white handkerchief, all cotton of course, thanks to Miss Picky Geena, and cursed under my breath. I didn't want the house staff to hear me.

I paced back and forth, hidden from sight and sound behind the heavy, gold brocade curtains I insisted on for the windows instead of the thin little white things Geena wanted. I was glad I insisted on them. At least they kept the sun out and much of the sometimes vicious, muggy Carolina heat we endured. She wanted to live near the ocean. Still, here was better than that damn desert!

How dare mother upbraid me! I shook my head bitterly. Sure she could. She believed she was a saint and I should behave like one too. After all, there was only one glaring downfall in her whole perfect, sanctimonious, famous life, of which I was the result.

I have had a few downfalls myself. Ramona was my first one as a professor, but there were more before and after her. I am that kind of man with those kinds of needs, and always will be. That doesn't mean I don't love my family greatly and well. Geena cares more about Celia and those damn misfits than she does about me. Simply put, I need to be first with her, and I am not. I hoped when we moved this far away from them, she would break her old habits, but no. After all, she moved here first.

She leaves me here alone all summer, so I travel. Then she insists I spend two weeks at Christmas with that store bunch. I wouldn't ever go back there except to please Mother, but she doesn't know that. Both Geena and Mother think I go for them. I don't. Bit I know where my bread needs buttering, and I know how to keep it buttered. I don't want Mother or William the Dude cutting me out of their wills. They have too much money for me to let that happen.

I better be careful. Very, very careful. Professors could easily lose their tenure over a couple of silly, short indiscretions with nondescript students who were only using me to get ahead anyway, so things were already risky with me. I didn't need this on top of that situation.

Thank God I travel a lot! That gives me the opportunity to leave any indiscretions behind and stay away long enough for it to be over with when I get back. So far, it works.

Geena. Mother. William the Dude. They were the important people I needed to pay attention to. I needed to do the necessary sorting out of this mess so I could see what each one required of me now. Whether I liked it or not or believed in what they thought, I knew they measured life differently than I did and always would. I hide that knowing from them, have for years, because I deserve a life too, with my own values running it, just like they do. They don't like the way I am, so I hide it from them. What else can I do?

I ran my hands through my hair and glanced in the mirror. I was still handsome. My hair is as black as night. I give myself an easy grin in the mirror. Mother is a famous artist. My guess is that Rose kept up with things so she could try and blackmail me. If I knew Mother, that wasn't going to happen!

Mother had spoken to me in that same cold monotone just once before. It was when one of the maids reported the girlie magazines hid under my bed to her back when I was a teenager. I wanted to shout at her. Who the hell did she think she was? Just one man, ever? She wanted to stay a righteous little virgin who had been wronged forever? And I was the spawn of that coupling? Of her undoing? Her mistake? Where was my father? She had plenty of money. She could hire someone to find him and make him toe the mark, like she did me. Maybe I wanted to meet him. All I knew was that he was an actor.

Actually, I never gave a damn. Not enough to ask her about him or to try to find him myself. I just want to keep the good life I have going without too many problems. So back then, I started hiding my way of being from them. I became very adept at fronting people off. Still am. I knew I was good looking and charming, and I came from a wealthy family with a famous artist for a mother. An only child. The Heir. I learned well how to hedge my bets.

I never looked back after Rose and I were through. She was a not very bright student of mine for a brief moment a few years ago. We were together a few times. Her name was pretty, and so was she. Tiny, slim, and childlike.

Outrage swept through me. How dare she try to do this do me! Why didn't she come forward before? I always took precautions with my women, so the kid obviously wasn't mine.

Mother said she would call me back in a few hours, after I got my head together, she said. Denial. That's all it took. I would stand my ground and shut up and let them figure it out.

Chapter Twenty One

Dreams?, I's gots' plenty dam' dreams
eber' nite' and all da' day long
readin' and a' pacin'
I takes' it out wid' ma' brushes
pour it to da' canvas
showin' what's a' hidin' in da' closet
me a knowing and dem' not, dat' it's a pair of skinny ankles
wid' red ribbons tied 'round dem' daincin' in high red heels
hoo haa !

Emma Makepeace

After speaking with Ray and informing him of the fact that he has a son, I hung up the phone. I looked around my upstairs bedroom, seeing it through angry, defensive eyes. It was the chaste bedroom of a virgin. Done in white, with creamy pinks and tans to soften the rigidity, it was distant and cool. It held no clue about the internal passion I suffered with day and night, and had, all of my life.

Didn't I have a right to take a personal, private stand about my life? The world believed I was a famous artist with a continental flair for travel and many passionate affairs. Well, I didn't. None. Zero. Except for my brief fling with Ray's father, I kept my passionate, romantic nature under lock and key.

Literally. My forbidden romance novels were hidden in their own private room, a part of my bedroom, in a room I kept under lock and key. Nobody except me knew the contents.

I unlocked the door, stepped inside and closed it. I looked around at the shelves neatly stacked with thousands of romance books. Always someone else's love story, never mine. Colorful, modern, lusty covers and sedate vintage Victoria Holts, her riotous romances hidden under her many pen names, Jane Austens, the Brontes, the Alcotts, Pierre Choderlos de Laclos, Henry James. A whole library hidden behind this door. A library of dreams and hopes and wishes, and yes, erotic tales of touch and heat.

I wandered over to my maroon reading chair and stroked its soft, velvety curves. I was very attached to its deep seat and wide arms. I glanced at the window. My habit was to pull the shades up when I read and pull them down when I left my secret room. I wasn't afraid of being seen so much as I valued the privacy of my second-floor quarters. My "closet," library measured twenty-five by eighteen feet.

The thoughts I was avoiding rushed in. Was Ray the way he was about women because I swore off of men after Barron disappeared? Was I too hurt, by Barron's flight when he found out I was with child that I somehow made life go wrong for my only child? It was true, I didn't understand men. Never did.

Barron was my first and only betrayal. My father raised me after mother died. I was too young to remember her. His constancy and kindness was always a part of my life. Father always cherished and protected my Sight and my sensitivities. I assumed all men were like him.

Should I have let Ray keep his own sort of library instead of telling him how disgusted I was with his hidden magazines and girlie books? I watched the closed look that came over his face back when he was a boy. Didn't some of my romance book collections come very close to the stuff in the books Ray hid back then?

I sighed, went out, closed the door and locked it. Ray inherited Barron's huge ego and good looks, but he was also a kind, good, albeit shortsighted man. What was I to do? I had to help him. I picked up the phone and called Gabe Butler, my lawyer.

"Gabe, I would appreciate you dropping by at your earliest convenience," I announced casually, after I finally got him on the phone. After a silence, during which he explored the meaning of my polite words, he said, "How soon?"

"Any time!" I snarled.

Oops! That was unexpected! I regained my composure while Gabe pondered my words for the depth of urgency contained in their meaning. He usually took this route with me, for being impeccably polite in front of people as introverts can be, I was even more impressive with innocent double entendres when in need.

"How about now?"

"That's best," I responded testily, and hung up before he could say any more. I swept out of my bedroom and ran down the stairs. Father stood at the bottom, watching me descend in a flurry of emotions and jerks. He caught me and held me when I reached him.

"Oh my God!" I shouted and started crying and laughing. He hastily pulled me into the downstairs library and closed the double doors. He waited until I could talk again.

"What's going on?"

"Oh, nothing," I answered in a high voice. I walked over to the writing table and sniffed the fresh, pale orange flowers. I studied the thousands of rare book titles rowed neatly behind glass doors, collected and organized by strangers, by staff. My real friends were hidden upstairs behind a closed, locked door in my bedroom.

I studied the ceiling. It was domed, painted with angel murals and images of saints. Large windows above and below let in light. Chairs and throws and plants in abundance were scattered pleasantly here and there. It was a large, elegant room, a library made for the reading of stately tomes, not for the reading of wild, sweet, secret romances. That kind of reading was meant for hidden rooms and summer meadows and deep woods.

Father waited until I regained my Equanimity. I had an emotional habit of writing the things down that affected me most deeply instead of speaking the words to him. I went to the huge, polished wood desk in the center of the library and wrote a note to my father. I knew it would change his world forever. Mine was already changed. I handed it to him and waited while he read it.

He shoved his hat back on his head and said, "Whew!" then rubbed his chin, like he always did. He grinned at me, and suddenly I laughed.

"We got a grandson? A great grandbaby?"

In a minute he said, "That fool boy!"

"Gabe is on his way here."

"We need a lawyer?"

"Fill me in," Father said, and began pacing the floor. He went to the door and shouted.

"Somebody bring us whiskey and some lemonade!"

A voice answered him from a distance. He shut the door and turned to me.

"First of all, this is our secret for now. Don't talk about it in front of anybody else until we figure it out."

I told him the simple truth.

"A woman named Rose Webb stopped here in an old pickup truck. She said she was one of Ray's students years ago. She said they had a brief affair, then he dumped her. She got pregnant, but she never told Ray because he was married. She dropped out of school and her folks threw her out when they found out. She ran away from home and stopped all contact with her relatives. She moved to California and raised their child there without any help or contact from her family or Ray. Now she is sick and needs our help."

"Is she terminally ill?"

"No. She packed up and drove here. I suppose to get away from whoever beat her up. She has been beat up and can't work right now. That's what she is calling sick. They don't have enough money to survive on."

I burst into tears.

"Maybe she's lying for money," Father said thoughtfully.

"No! She isn't! He's seven and the spitting image of Ray at that age!'

"He was with her?" Father said wonderingly.

"Yes!"

I waited a moment before I told him the rest.

"They're here. In the Holly House."

The Holly House was one of three guest houses on the property. Father grinned again, but his face had gone white with the tumbling shock of all of this news at once. The whiskey and lemonade came just then, and I anxiously ordered sandwiches, soup and cake to be brought to us immediately. Betty looked at us questioningly and backed out the door.

"Aw heck! All I need is a Stroh's beer!" Father sputtered. But I knew better.

"I don't know whether to celebrate or cry," I said.

"Maybe both," he said.

I went to a window and looked out. It was summer, but I wished the snow was flying, coming down and covering us with cold and calm. The Shadow. It was back again. This time with gifts that could be shunned or welcomed. My son had an illegitimate child. I would do nothing to hurt my grandson. Celia's half-brother.

"I want to show you something before Gabe gets here," I told Father after he ate, and his color came back. He followed me up the stairs and into my bedroom. I locked the door behind us and opened my library closet.

"Come inside," I said.

He walked in, looked around, and let out a low whistle.

"You mean you been keeping all of this stifled up here?"

I started crying.

"I didn't mean any harm! Remember when I chewed Ray out about his girlie magazines and took them away from him? You told me to let him be, that he was just being a boy, but I wouldn't listen to you. Ray might have some kind of womanizer complex because of me!"

Father laughed.

"He was just being a college boy back then. Now will you listen to me? I know men better than you do. Ray is not the first one to fool around in school, and he won't be the last. But when he got married, the whole story changed. He made a commitment to Geena, and to her only. I know he strays, but that's another story. Let's not make it part of this one. He's completely responsible for his antics, not us, and we are not going to get into that part of it. Does he know? What did he say about it?"

I nodded. "He knows. I called him earlier. He had no shame or any curiosity about the child or concern for the mother. Just frustration that his perfect life might be ruined, or his professorship put in danger."

I threw my hands in the air.

"He was only angry on his own behalf."

I felt a mother's helpless bitterness at a child's willful wrongdoing.

"Did I cause him to be so selfish?"

"No." Father answered my question with certainty. "That's just Ray. He's more like Barron than you."

He took a deep breath.

"I guess we'll just have to handle this ourselves."

He looked me in the eye.

"You know I'm right."

Reluctantly I nodded. He spoke with decision and authority. I was relieved of my predicament as a failed mother with his soothing words. Father always had a knack for setting my world right again. That gift was needed more than once. Father started me painting as a way to express the passion that so easily could have become violence, or a death wish within me after Barron deserted me. Ray has the same passion. I kept mine trapped inside until father showed me the way out. Instead of writing, I paint. And read romance novels. I closed my secret library door, locked it, and we went downstairs.

I thought to wait for Gabe in the library, but Father had other ideas. He wanted to meet "Ray".

I corrected him.

"This child's name is Rayfield, last name Webb. I don't know if he has a middle name...our grandson."

"If he's about nine, then he is four years older than Celia."

Father thought that one over. Then he sighed.

"Okay! Let's go do it."

I left orders with Betty to have Gabe wait in the library. We walked to the Holly House holding each other's hands for support. We knocked on the door and went in. They sat scrunched up tight against each other on one end of a sofa. We walked toward them and stopped when they both waved us away.

"This was a really bad idea," Rose said.

The boy looked thin and malnourished. He was the image of Ray. He nodded fearfully, his black eyes so much like Rays.

"We should get on the road now."

They slid off of the sofa and stood up. Rose was swaying on her feet, tiny, tough, slim, and bruised all over. The boy wrapped an arm around her.

"Let's go, mom," he said, steering her toward us bravely.

"Why don't you both stay awhile? Take a load off your feet. The road will still be out there waiting for you two when you're ready," father persuaded in a soft voice.

"You're not taking me away from my mom," the boy stated flatly.

"No. I was wrong to come here. You will try to take him away from me because he is Ray's son."

Rose put a shaky hand to her forehead. I stepped forward.

"You need some rest," instead of saying that she needed a doctor.

"Nobody's going to take anybody away from anybody around here," father stated. The boy stopped and gave him a weary look, as if to say that he was too tired to think about anything. Both of them weaved back and forth. Father held out his arms to Ray's child. I edged toward Rose and soon held her in my arms.

I watched with tears streaming down my face as a little lost boy's arms stole around his grandfather's neck. Their faces will be etched forever in my mind and I knew that someday I would paint them.

Father picked him up, carried him to the sofa and sat down with him. The boy sighed and tucked his head into Father's plaid shirt, exhausted, hiding his face from the world. Ray did the same thing when he was young. Young Ray had a protector now, wanted or not.

These two souls were starved for much more than just food, but that would have to be a start. I called the main house to have Betty bring food to the guest house. I told the staff to use the kitchen entrance and leave the food and drinks on the counter. Betty would call me when Gabe got here and I would call the doctor to come out later today. When I was done, I flew back to the living room on winged feet and sat with Rose, my grandson, and my father.

Gabe was late, but that was good. It gave us the chance to get a little bit used to each other. I decided to spring Gabe on them, and hopefully, his knowledge as a lawyer would end their fear of being stolen by us.

But they clammed up as soon as they met him. I could tell that Rose thought she had entered a nightmare. That the lawyer was here to take Rayfield away from her. Her eyes widened with horror at what she thought was her mistake. She clutched Rayfield and planned her flight.

I watched it happening and knew I couldn't stop it. I excused myself and ran back to the main house. Rose believed I was going to get someone else to help take her child away from her. She was worried about being locked up or dying. She was getting ready to run for her life again.

I ran to the office, locked the door behind me, and opened the wall safe. I took out all the cash and looked around for something to put it in. There was a small blue and red vase on the table with polished pebbles in it. I closed the safe and locked it, emptied the vase and stuffed the money in it. Then I scribbled a note with an address on it, stuffed it in the vase, and fled. I ran outside to Rose's old beat up truck, laid the vase in the middle of the seat, slammed the truck door shut and rushed back to the guest house. Rose was standing, Rayfield clutched in her arms, slowly inching her way towards the front door.

"Father!" I said, to get his attention.

"Gabe! Stop! Rose has to leave this time!"

I ran over to Rose and Rayfield and started hugging and kissing on them. They didn't push me away. The hugs and kisses landed here and there. I didn't care where.

"Father, if you want any loving, you better get started!"

I laughed through my tears. Father froze. He was deciding whether to fight this or not. Then he gave in and rushed us. Gabe shut up and wisely, stayed out of the way.

Rose kept moving. She couldn't do anything different than she was doing. She couldn't let herself have us yet, and there was nothing I could to do about it right now. I didn't want what a court battle would cost them and us.

I wasn't sure this was the right way to handle this situation, but it's what my instincts told me were right. Father usually let me have my way in these things, for they almost always came out right. We kissed and hugged on them and told them sweet love things until they were back in the old truck again.

"Look in the vase!"

I shouted through the window at her as she drove away. I turned to Father. We crumbled into each other's arms and watched them until they were out of sight. We swayed in place like lilies in a strong wind. I don't know how long it was before Gabe spoke.

"Why don't you two come in the house and have something to drink?"

I ran back to the guest house, knowing something had been left there. In the corner of the sofa lay a cheap little green figure of a soldier. I laughed and ran back out to Father, holding it in my hand. I gave it to him.

"Keep this for our grandson, for when he comes back. He'll want it then."

I spoke with confidence and knowing. Father's tears stopped at my words. Hope flooded his face. He held the little toy up and looked it over. Then he cleared his throat and took a stance about the whole thing.

"I'll do it," he said, and tucked the little soldier in his shirt pocket. He put his arm around my shoulder. We wove our way toward the house.

"I put all the money from the safe and the address of the monastery in the vase. I hope they will go there."

Father whistled. "All of it?"

"There wasn't much. I was getting ready to replenish it when this happened. I put a note in with the money telling them to go to the monastery."

"Good."

He nodded.

Chapter Twenty Two

Boy's n' gals, I got troubles agin'
troubles' gonna' gimme da' blues
day' tryin' ta' make me feel bad
agin' bout' my womens' and chiles'
well, dat' ain't no new news.

Ray Makepeace

The damned idiots didn't call until the next morning. They called early, the worst time of the day for me. The time when I never at my best at planning things. They said Rose and the kid had come and gone. They gave her some money, she left. That was it. No one was to know anything about it except for us three and Gabe. They would handle the situation from here on out. Geena and her mother and Celia, none of the rest needed to know anything about it. They told me to stay out of it.

I let them talk. I was relieved. I knew how they worked from past experience. They figured it all out probably within minutes after being presented with the problem. They were both short with me. They said very little, just the facts, then hung up. I knew they would stay mad at me for a while, but then they would forgive me. That was our pattern.

I didn't ask about the boy. Maybe the kid was my son, maybe not. Geena couldn't have more children. That was fine with me. Mother and William the Dude would sort this problem out and take care of it "as needed."

They were old and needed something to handle anyway. I never gave them any obvious trouble before. Nothing they needed to know about. Besides, I wasn't the first guy and I won't be the last one to get mixed up with hookers. Maybe I had better err on the side of caution though. At least for awhile. Having a secure, unruffled marriage is a big plus to a professor's career. Maybe I should call Geena today. See how everything is out there in the desert for her and Celia. I never worry about Geena being unfaithful to me. That's the least of my worries. Mine are more about trying to keep her home and my little clandestine meetings hidden.

I stared out the dining room window at the expanse of green, rolling lawn. The sprinklers came on. I thought about how Geena loved me. So pure and so true. She was the only woman I would ever love, but I could never let her know that. If I did, she would gain the upper hand with me. Like Mother once had. It was better this way.

I put my coffee cup down and stood up. It was highly irritating to have to watch the sprinklers going back and forth in their monotonous routine while I was having breakfast. It was time to speak to the garden staff about a new sprinkling schedule.

Ćhapter Twenty Three

We' gonna' eat our Sunday dinner
take a restin' seat on the front porch
fan the heat away after the matter is rectified,
ya' young cur dog in heat, and don't ya' try
bein' uppity with us, or we'll whip yore' ass...fast!

Emma and William the Dude, Tom and Dan

"Okay. That's done." William put the phone down. He finished talking to Ray. He and Emma stared at each other in silence. Then William cleared his throat.

"I guess it's time to call Tom and let him know he might or might not be having a couple more guests show up at the monastery."

Emma nodded and before he turned away to call the monastery, William said, "Go paint something, darlin'."

Emma nodded. Her mind filled with the colors she would use to paint her disappointment in Ray and her elation at discovering her grandson. She left him talking on the phone and went to her studio. She took her time, the things she was feeling required it. She set up a blank canvas in her studio, grateful to William for handling what she could not. She looked around her studio. This place. She owned it. She was its master. And it responded to the new, empty canvas with bleak shades of blue and angry shades of red.

William hung up the phone and went to Emma's studio.

"I'm going to the store," he announced.

"What for?"

"I think we need to call in Dan Swain to track Rose and Rayfield for us. Of course, we won't tell anyone, but we will need Timmon's help to get his phone number."

Emma cleaned her brush and laid it down.

"I'm going with you."

*

Brother Tom watched them through a front window. The old blue truck inched up the long driveway and stopped. He opened the front door and watched the woman and boy get out of the truck and stand there, staring at him with fear filled faces. He held out his arms in a wide, welcoming gesture and spoke loud, hearty words to bridge the gap between them.

"Welcome! William and Emma said you would be coming! We are so glad to welcome you to our monastery where your privacy and security is guaranteed. We have a small house ready for you. It's private and on the lake. No one will bother you there.

You can come and go as you please, although we do provide meals and everything else here. And you can stay as long as you want to. It's our own little world, and we only let in who we want in. William and Emma have been coming here for years on retreat."

He kept on talking as he inched closer to them. Suddenly the woman threw up her hand in a gesture of defeat.

"Can you hide us from him? He's good at finding us."

Brother Tom looked her over. She didn't say his name. He would try for it later. She was skinny, small and covered with bruises. He looked at the boy. He looked physically okay. Brother Tom knew all about emotional abuse. He wondered briefly about the depth of the emotional battering the boy had taken.

"Yes. We sure can."

Brother Tom spoke with restraint while his kind heart surged with sympathy. He wanted to get his ham fists on whoever did this to these two. He wanted to tower over that man and pound the fear of God into him. Afraid that the woman might sense his surge of violence, he quickly pushed the thought away.

"Mind if I take a look at your truck?" he asked in a gentle voice. No need to sound like an inquisitor, which he could when necessary.

"Okay."

He rubbed his hands together, smiling with anticipation as he hurried to the faded blue truck. The truck was a half-ton 1951 Advance Design Chevy with vent windows in the doors, an eighty MPH speedometer and chrome window handle knobs. Brother Tom unlatched and lifted the hood and looked under it while Rose and Ray watched him. It was on its last legs. He kept talking.

"We have an auto repair shop right here on the property," he announced to them in a pleased voice. "The brothers running it would love to get their hands on this jewel."

He closed the hood and nodded to them.

"I expect you want a tour of the monastery before you see your place?? We have a chapel if you want to join us for worship. It's behind the main house and offices."

He gestured at the graceful building.

"The hours are posted in the main room."

He shrugged.

"Not something you are required to do, only if you want to."

They followed him to the little white house just past the last cabin by the lake. He stood around waiting until they looked it over.

"Okay to send Brother French over to assist with any...ahhh... medicines or medical help you might need? He's our resident doc."

Rose sighed. "Okay."

Brother Tom hurried back to the main building. Before long, the refrigerator and cupboards in the small house were stocked with food and there were two good, well used bicycles resting against the front porch. The gates to the monastery were locked, and the truck was in the auto repair shop. Brother French, the doctor, had seen to Miss Rose, and she was sleeping. Ray was playing board games with two of the Brothers.

Brother Tom picked up the phone and dialed a number.

"They are here," he said into the phone. Wild sobbing greeted his announcement. He waited while William took the phone from Emma.

"They are here," he announced again.

"Well, dog my cats," William said after a silence.

"Good."

"Are they okay?"

Brother Tom, who was used to William's way of talking, filled him in.

"Rose is sleeping. Brother French says she will be just fine. Rayfield is playing board games and eating Oreos, Twinkies, Cheese Whiz and crackers."

"Good."

After a while, Brother Tom said, "She wants us to hide her and Ray from someone. I don't know who yet or how dangerous they might be. But she has been beaten up before, I think, and she said, 'he always finds us.'"

Silence hummed along the phone line while both men digested the situation and its possibilities.

"Well, we called in Dan Swain, a private eye. He's going to start tracking him as soon as we get a name. Try to get it from her, okay? The sooner the better."

"I'll call you tomorrow," Brother Tom said.

"Good."

William hung up and turned to Emma.

Out loud he said, "Our grandson is eating every snack food known to mankind and playing board games with the Brothers. Rose has been tended to, and she is sleeping. Brother Tom put them in the little white house just past the last cabin on the lake. You know the one. He has posted guards at the entry and the gates are closed. Now go get some rest. You haven't eaten or slept in two days."

"I wonder who's after them?"

"Don't worry about it right now. Just go get some rest."

William was weary with both elation and worry. It was time for a catnap. Too much excitement always wore a man's sorry ass out. He would finance an even more elaborate security system, electronics and all, at the monastery if they stayed there. He would think it over later.

"Boy, sometimes when it rains, it pours," he muttered to himself, mopping his forehead with his large red bandana, remembering the surprise visit from the "Three Magi" at the store just a few short weeks ago.

He had diverted them to the monastery, too. He and Emma never spoke of the great loss they endured a short time before the Three Magi showed up. A loss that plunged both of them into a steady, never ending sorrow until this new, innocent rebirth dropped in on them, forging their sorrow into a mix of elation and new hope.

"Maybe Heaven is a place on Earth. I sure hope so for all of us. Dudeism, don't fail me now."

He stopped muttering and took a long swallow of whiskey. Algestine's fruitcake wasn't available right now, so whiskey was the best he could do. His heart lurched with emotion and steadied. He wandered toward a large chair, collapsed into it and fell asleep almost instantly. His last thought before sleep was that it was a bitch getting old. Caused you to lose old friends and lose out on a whole bunch of raising hell.

These days he had to assign the whippings and the dancing to other people. Damn it all to hell!

Chapter Twenty Four

You's a sinna', ain't no doubt
I knows' ya' cain't seem ta' work it out
but here's the thaing ya' see
ever body's blues bout' cha'
done been fallin' back on me

Emma Makepeace

She stared out the window at the sunshine bathing the desert. Her thoughts turned to Geena in irritation. She had tried to get Geena to go to Europe with her before, but no, stubborn, obtuse Geena followed Ray around instead. She wanted her to meet Barron's Swift's ancestors so she could understand why Ray was the way he was before she found out about his cheating. Barron came from a long line of people who survived on haughtiness, pretenses, and numerous affairs. Ray was just following their genetic lead. She sighed and turned away from the window and went to the phone.

*

The ringing phone woke him. He scowled at it. Grudgingly he picked it up. It was too early for any decent human to be calling him. Certainly whoever it was would get a piece of his mind. Unless it was Geena with an emergency or something. His wife did have a propensity for making mountains out of molehills.

"Hello," he stated abruptly, businesslike.

"I want to you get two golden retriever puppies for the girls before they get home. Do it right away so the dogs can get used to your staff. And you."

"What?"

"This is your mother, Ray, and I intend for the girls to have two golden retriever puppies waiting for them when they return. Do you understand? Say they are from you."

A long silence rolled down the phone line as he digested her latest punishment of him.

"Okay. But why?"

"Do you really need to ask, son?"

"No, I guess not. You have some kind of reason that probably makes sense to you, so I will do it. It won't be easy, though, because I am gone so much for extended periods of time."

"Don't go Professor on me, Ray. I'm your mother. I know your house staff, and they will be happy to take care of the dogs and show them love and respect, whether you're there or not. No more excuses. I expect a call from you as soon as the puppies are brought home. Make it very soon."

She started to hang up on him then she changed her mind and whispered into the mouthpiece.

"They desperately need someone to love that can love them back. And they are not trying to find it in the embraces of students that look and dress like emaciated teeny boppers. They are trying to find it in you. That's why they need the dogs, son. Oh. And

don't name them. That's for Geena and Celia to do."
She laid the phone back in its cradle.

Book Three in the Desert Store Series
The Three Cactus Limbo
Bud's Garage and the Quest of the Three Magi

Bud Spinner is a fear filled, reclusive garage owner living on the outskirts of Ardenville, a shy inner knower of hidden Goodness in people. He helps Map Girl and Geena escape Ardenville with cash and a map. Bud yearns to leave, too. He secretly writes auto manuals, banking the money in a town away from Ardenville. Bud can repair any classic car ever made. A loner, he makes friends with Ben and Andy, two other fear filled recluses who also fly under the radar in Ardenville. Both have mechanical engineering degrees and work in the town factory. Ben reads science fiction. Andy fishes unsuccessfully.

The three men appear to be boring, aging bachelors to the citizens of Ardenville, but each one carries abilities inside they instinctively keep hidden from the citizens of Ardenville.

Unknown to themselves as well as to the town, they are spiritualists who sense good or evil in others. They detect emotions and intentions, and constantly stay on overwhelm from it. Extremely resistant to the ills of the outside world, their solution is to hide.

They buy a cabin and settle for weekends away from Ardenville. But Dan, a private eye hired by Mama to keep tabs on her ex, ejects them from their cabin, and they flee Ardenville to deliver a gift to Map Girl.

Three older roadies who have never been roadies before, traveling in their classic cars, heading for Cowboy Johnson's store, a monastery and the ocean. A story of waking up and allowing the hidden Goodness of life to happen.

CPSIA information can be obtained
at www.ICGtesting.com
Printed in the USA
LVHW090011010820
662068LV00012B/441